Pink

J.K. Bruce

HEMBURY
BOOKS

About the author

Originally from England, J K Bruce's diverse work history informs her powerful storytelling. Leaving school at sixteen, she explored various paths, from filing letters in a bank to walking the wards of Latrobe Valley Hospital as a social worker. For seventeen years, she shared her expertise at a local TAFE college, teaching disability, aged care and community health.

As a novelist, Bruce draws inspiration from her surroundings – her first book, *Into the Dying Forest*, is set in the vibrant landscapes surrounding her home in West Gippsland. Bruce's new novel, *Pink*, set in 1960s Melbourne, is a love story which interrogates themes of Catholic guilt, social expectations of women and the long term impact of trauma.

Currently living on a rural property overlooking a forest, Bruce dedicates her time to writing books, reading fiction and nonfiction, and creating a haven for local wildlife.

First published by Hembury Books in 2025

hemburybooks.com.au

info@hemburybooks.com

ISBN 9781923517264 (paperback)

ISBN 9781923517257(ebook)

A catalogue record for this book is available from the National Library of Australia

In loving memory of David W Bruce,
husband and father.

Chapter One

1966

On a hot Monday morning in early February, Jo Kelly, aged eighteen, caught the train from Noble Park to the city. She wore a pink shift that finished four inches above her knees and her legs were bare. Her mum said she looked cheap, but her mum was old-fashioned.

The carriage was nearly full and smelt of cigarette smoke. Most of the passengers crouched behind copies of *The Sun*, but a couple of men were giving Jo the eye. Her dark hair fell below her shoulders, and she sat with her legs crossed, revealing a strip of bare thigh. Lighting a cigarette, she stared through the grimy window as houses, shopping strips and factories flashed past. *You're beautiful*, Robert had said, before they screwed for the first time. She'd thought he meant it, but she'd been a fool. He hadn't called for weeks, even when she was in hospital. Now, the rest of her life stretched ahead, as desolate as the surface of the moon.

The train rumbled into Flinders Street and screeched to a stop. Jo stepped onto the platform, joining the crowd moving towards the escalator that took them up to the main part of the station. She walked past the tea and pie stands towards the entrance, where buckets of bright flowers stood opposite the ticket offices, and down the broad flight of steps to the street. Crossing at the lights, she walked along Swanston Street and turned into Collins, going past the old stone churches and Karl of Switzerland's model academy to Coates Building, a fourteen-storey glass tower next to the solid mass of the Melbourne Club.

On the sixth floor of Coates Building a row of bored-looking girls lounged in the corridor outside Sylvia's Secretarial College. Next to the college stood the door to Douglas Lang and Co., Importers. Jo opened it and walked past the switchboard into the girls' room, a small area smelling of perfume and hair spray, with a rack for coats and a collection of umbrellas in a wastepaper bin.

As she peered at her reflection in the mirror, the door opened and her friend Ruth hurried in, brown-eyed and anxious, a cane basket hooked over her arm.

'How was your weekend?' Ruth asked, plonking her basket on the floor.

Jo made a face. 'Another fun time in front of the telly.'

Ruth stared at her. 'I hope you're not staying home because of Robert.'

'I'm too tired to go out,' Jo said. Only four weeks ago, she'd been lying in a hospital bed, a black rubber tube hanging out of her side.

Ruth's nose wrinkled. 'My weekend was awful too. Mum went to Castlemaine, so I had to work in the milk bar.'

'Poor us,' Jo said. She took one last look at herself and went out into the main office, which was cluttered with desks and filing cabinets. Three glass cubicles stood in front, all occupied by men.

Jo's desk butted up to a wall of grimy windows with views of rooftops and washing lines. Her chair creaked as she sat down. Another boring day loomed ahead. Sometimes, she wondered if she should train to be a nurse, or a teacher, but she hated the sight of blood and the only kid she knew was bratty Simone, who was going to be a flower girl at Maureen's wedding. Maureen, Jo's big sister, was marrying Michael in October.

Right now, Jo couldn't think of anything worse than being a bridesmaid at Maureen's wedding.

Up ahead, Mr Cleary, the chief accountant, emerged from the executives' suite and walked towards her desk. He was over six feet tall and wore a navy pin-striped suit.

'Jo, would you please come to my office,' he said.

Jo's stomach fluttered as she stood up. Had she done something wrong? She followed Mr Cleary past the glass cubicles and along the plush carpeted corridor that led to the executive suites. Mr Cleary walked with long strides, so it was difficult to keep up. His office was filled with an oversized desk and looked out over Collins Street. At one side stood a silver framed photo of his wife and three kids – all boys, with shy smiles and short haircuts – and in front three orange glass paperweights an equal distance apart.

'Have a seat,' Mr Cleary said.

Jo sat down and crossed her legs, her pink shift high on her thighs while Mr Cleary folded himself into his chair, his hands on the desk. Dark hairs sprouted from their backs.

'Paul is, er, leaving us,' Mr Cleary said. 'I think you're quite bright, so I'm offering you Paul's job.'

Jo's eyes opened wider. *Quite bright.* At school she'd been in the top five percent.

'Well?' Mr Cleary asked. 'What do you say?'

She swallowed. 'Thank you, Mr Cleary.'

'You'll take it?'

'Yes,' she said.

Mr Cleary smiled. 'I think you'll manage just fine. Paul is leaving on Friday, but he'll show you what to do. Your new rate of pay begins today. You'll be reporting directly to me.'

'Thank you,' Jo said again. Out of the blue, she'd been given a promotion to a job previously held by a man. She wished she could boast about it to Robert, who thought he was smarter than her because he was an engineering student. *Bastard.*

Paul scowled when she walked into his cubicle.

'You've accepted the job,' he said in a dry voice. 'I didn't know you had accounting experience.'

'I don't,' Jo said.

Paul's lip curled. 'You know Cleary's being a cheapskate, don't you? You'll be working a man's job for a woman's pay.'

'Mr Cleary said you'd show me what to do,' Jo said as politely as she could.

Paul frowned. 'We won't get much done by Friday, but it'll have to do. Go grab your chair.'

Jo walked over to her desk, watched by Nola from the typing pool. Nola was the oldest woman in the office, over forty, and unmarried.

At morning teatime, cups and saucers rattled as the tea lady, wearing a neck-to-knee apron over her dress, wheeled her loaded trolley into the office. Jo stood up. 'I'll be back after morning tea.'

'Ten minutes,' Paul said, obviously begrudging her the time.

Jo took her chair back to her desk and sat down. She'd just lit a cigarette when Nola came over. One of her eyes had a cast; it seemed to peer over Jo's shoulder as she said, 'Congratulations on getting Paul's job. It's a step up for you.' Nola's smile vanished. 'You won't get Paul's cubicle if that's what you're thinking. They're reserved for the men. It's better if we girls stick together, one big happy family.'

Jo tilted her head and blew out smoke. What a joke. Every female in the office was ranked in a pecking order based on whether they were married, engaged or going steady. Nola was at the bottom. To compensate, she'd become the office prefect.

'I don't want Paul's cubicle,' Jo said.

Nola gave a satisfied nod. 'Good. We girls need to know our place.'

Jo stared after Nola as she marched back to her desk. What a load of rubbish. She could do Paul's job better than him any day.

…

At six o'clock in the afternoon, Jo emerged from the Noble Park railway station. A few eucalyptus trees grew at the edge of the car park and the air smelt of dust. On the opposite side of the road stood a corner milk bar hung with Peters Ice Cream and Four'N Twenty pie signs, Steve the Greek's fish and chips, a faded haberdashery and the shining window of Charles Payne, Criminal Barrister and Solicitor. Except for Charles Payne's office, everything had looked the same for years.

Crossing the road, Jo walked past the service station and workshop where Michael, her future brother-in-law worked, and Noble Park Tech, a huddle of low buildings at the top of a rise. Seven minutes later she arrived in a new housing estate of triple-fronted brick veneers. Mather Road appeared; the pampas grass at her parents' front gate rippled in the wind. She clattered up the path towards the concrete porch, edged by her mother's carefully tended roses. Inside, the heat hit her like a wave along with the smell of grilled lamb chops. Rufus rushed down the hall, his pink tongue hanging out. She bent down and fondled his ears. 'Hello, hot boy.'

'I'm home,' she called.

No-one answered. Rufus followed her into the bedroom she shared with Maureen and flopped onto the carpet. Two beds almost filled the space and Maureen's glory box, an intricately carved cedar chest with a brass clasp was pushed against Jo's record player. The cedar chest was stuffed with sheets, blankets and towels, and engagement presents filled the cardboard boxes piled on top of the wardrobe and under Maureen's bed.

Jo put The Righteous Brothers onto the turntable and started to undress.

Banging sounded on the other side of the wall. 'Stop that noise,' her younger sister Kathleen yelled. 'I'm doing my homework.'

Jo stuck out her tongue and took the record off. Wearing her undies, she went over to the mirror and stared at herself in the glass. Her hips stuck out like jug handles and two dark red scars marked her right side, one crescent shaped, the other a thick wedge. She pulled a face. Her body was ruined. She'd just finished pulling on a pair of shorts and a top when her mum's voice came along the hall. 'Tea's ready.'

Jo took a last look at herself in the mirror and went into the kitchen.

Her mum, Monica, stood at the counter in a print dress, dishing up the tea, her forehead glistening with sweat. In her wedding photo she was pretty, but now she looked old and bad tempered. 'Go call your father, will you?' Monica said.

Jo went to the back door, yelled 'Tea's ready,' at the open garage door then headed for the kitchen. The front door banged, and Maureen arrived in her black salon clothes, her long hair dyed strawberry blonde and perfectly styled, then Kathleen with her swimmer's shoulders and clear gaze that could spot hypocrites and fakes with ease. ('Robert's too full of himself to care about you,' she'd told Jo. 'Get rid of him.')

They sat around the table, their plates piled with lamb chops, mashed potatoes and peas.

'Say grace, please,' Monica said to the girls' dad.

Everyone bowed their heads as Kev muttered a few words and waited until he'd taken his first mouthful before they began to eat.

Monica poured herself a glass of water. 'A woman came in for a fitting today, and her breasts were almost down to her waist. I'd never seen anything like it. And here's me with nothing.'

Jo had seen her mum's breasts lots of times. They were disgusting, almost flat, studded with dark red nipples the size of a teat on a baby's bottle.

Maureen scooped up some mashed potato. 'You'd think she'd have an operation.'

'It would probably cost too much,' Monica said. 'But I did manage to get her a decent fitting bra. She was very pleased. Walked out of the shop with a smile on her face.'

'That's fab,' Maureen said.

Kev picked up a chop and gnawed at the bone.

Monica glared at him but said nothing.

'I got a new job and a pay rise today,' Jo said. Instantly she regretted it. Her board might go up.

'How much?' Maureen asked.

'Ten dollars a week.'

'What's the job?' Monica asked.

'Accounts clerk,' Jo said. 'Paul did it before me.'

Kev's blue eyes twinkled behind his glasses. 'Congratulations, love.'

Jo smiled at him. 'Thanks, Dad.'

'Fab,' Kathleen said.

Monica frowned. 'Don't be too pleased with yourself. Men don't like clever girls.'

Jo stabbed a pea with her fork.

'I've chosen the wedding invitations,' Maureen said.

Monica's face lit up. 'The scrolled border or the plain?'

'The scrolled,' Maureen said, 'with a bow at the top.'

'Lovely.'

Jo and Kathleen shared a look. Maureen and Michael's wedding was the most important thing in their mum's life. Nothing else seemed to matter.

Chapter Two

The following Saturday Ian sat with Elaine in Pellegrini's, at the top of Bourke Street. She was petite and blonde; he was broad-shouldered with a wide brow and jaw. Elaine's bright green dress clung to her curves. He found it hard to take his eyes off the hollow between her breasts.

They ate a seafood grill and Italian salad. During the meal, Elaine seemed nervous, taking large gulps from her glass of wine.

'Is something the matter?' Ian asked.

Elaine glanced at him and looked away. 'I don't think we have a future,' she said quietly.

His jaw dropped. There'd been no warning this was coming.

'We've been going out for a year, and we're not getting anywhere,' she said.

He'd been stupid not to see it. She wanted marriage and kids. He leaned towards her. 'You're the only woman in my life,' he said.

Her bottom lip trembled. 'I want someone who's prepared to commit.'

Ian reached for her hand, but she pulled it away. 'Is it that you don't want to marry again, or you don't want to marry *me*?'

'I don't want to marry again,' Ian said.

Elaine's eyes filled with tears. Strands of hair had unravelled from her French roll and hung around her ears, making her look younger than twenty-six. 'Well, that's it, then. I'm going home. Don't try to contact me. I won't change my mind.'

His chest hollowed out. She was leaving him. 'Stay,' he said. 'Please. We need to talk.'

'Why?' Elaine asked. 'You've made your position very clear.'

'Look,' he said, 'I'm being honest. I care about you. Doesn't that count for anything?

Elaine shook her head. 'No, because you won't commit.'

Her chair scraped the floor as she stood up and headed for the door. Ian watched her open it and walk outside. For a moment he imagined running after her, going down on his knees on the pavement. *Please, don't leave me.* A pulse beat in his throat. If he did that he was trapped.

He paid for their meal and caught the number 67 tram home. As the tram rattled along St Kilda Road, images of Elaine swirled through his head. How she threw back her head when she laughed. Naked, in his bed.

He'd met her at the sandwich bar near his workplace one lunchtime. She'd been standing in front of him waiting to be served. His eyes had lingered on the back of her slender neck, where her hair was swept up into a French roll, and the zip of her dress, which went all the way down to the gentle curve of her bum. When she opened her purse, she dropped some coins. He'd bent down and picked them up, offering them to her with a smile. She was as pretty at the front as she was from behind. She'd smiled back.

They'd gone to bed on their second date. Elaine didn't seem to mind that Ange got most of his pay, and what was left disappeared into the pockets of his landlord, Italian grocery shops, and the South Melbourne market. Elaine was a secretary, on a good salary for a woman. They'd argued once when she'd offered to pay her share of a restaurant bill. He'd refused, annoyed that she thought he couldn't afford it. A man paid for his girl.

Back home in his flat, the air felt too warm, and the venetians were open. Lights gleamed from the surrounding flats and the tortuous shape of a gnarled old tree rose into a sky reflecting the night glow of the city. He switched on the light. The room was furnished with pieces he'd scrouged from nature strips and generous friends – a dark red couch, kidney-shaped coffee table, a TV with rabbit ears. When Ange threw him out, he'd taken just his clothes, the cardboard boxes of the detective and science fiction stories he'd collected since he was a teenager, his record player and records. His record player sat on top of a second-hand sideboard next to a photo of his daughter Anna, and his books lined the shelves of a battered bookcase.

He'd tidied the room earlier, expecting Elaine would be here, but instead of being welcoming it looked sad and empty. Only the photo of Anna gave him comfort. Closing the venetians, he went into his bedroom. Stripping to his underpants, he left his jacket, shirt and pants on the floor. His arms and shoulders had plenty of muscle, and a fuzz of dark hair on his chest ran in a line to his navel. Scratching his belly, he wandered into the kitchen and drank a couple of glasses of water. Maybe he'd been wrong to be so honest with Elaine, but after his divorce he'd vowed to have no more lies in his life. He went into the living room and put Peggy Lee onto his turntable. Sitting on the couch, he let the music wash through him.

...

A week later Ian's EH Holden slid to a stop outside the house in Werribee that he'd shared with Ange. The front door opened and Anna skipped out, rosy cheeked, carrying a small bag. It would hold her pyjamas, change of underwear and socks, blue rabbit and a tattered piece of blanky that she liked to stroke as she fell asleep. Ian felt a wave of love as she came down the path. He opened the passenger door and she climbed inside, leaning towards him for a kiss. Her dark wavy hair brushed his cheek.

He threw her bag onto the back seat, put on the indicator and pulled out into the street.

'How's school?' he asked.

'Good,' Anna said. 'Did you get me a new colouring book?'

Ian nodded. 'And more coloured pencils.'

Anna wriggled back into her seat. 'Goody. Are we seeing Elaine?'

'No, sweetie.'

Anna made a face. 'I like Elaine.' She added, 'Mummy's got a new boyfriend. He bought me a doll, but I wanted a rabbit. Can I have a rabbit, please Daddy?'

You couldn't keep a rabbit in a flat all day. The place would stink.

'When I have a backyard,' Ian said.

Anna pouted. 'But I want one now.'

'You'll have to ask Mummy.'

'She said no.'

Anna's face wore her obstinate expression. 'If you won't buy me a rabbit, I'm gonna ask Grandma.'

Ian grinned. 'Good luck.'

...

Ian's mum, Mary, lived in Alphington in a narrow street of weatherboard houses next to the railway line. When Ian pulled up outside her house, she was watering her roses with a hose. She was a short woman in a flowered dress with a head of thick grey hair and a placid expression that concealed the fact she'd had a hard time with his father. She looked over and waved as they got out of the car.

The old wrought iron gate squeaked as Ian pushed it open and he and Anna walked up the path. Some of the roses were flowering in pink, yellow and peach; their faint scent hung in the still air.

Mary turned off the tap and bent down to give Anna a hug. 'This is a pleasant surprise. Just as well I made a sponge cake this morning.'

Anna's eyes shone. 'Has it got passionfruit icing?'

'You can't have a sponge cake without passionfruit icing,' Mary said. 'And, lucky for you, I've got a bottle of lemonade in the fridge.'

Her eyes met Ian's over Anna's head. It was a game she played with Anna every time they visited. She didn't get to see Anna as often as Ange's mother, but Ian was glad that she never complained. He felt guilty enough already.

They went into the house. A small table with a dried flower arrangement stood in the hall, and grey floral carpet stretched from the front door to the back verandah. Nothing had changed since Ian was a kid.

They walked down the hall to the kitchen, where pale green cupboards lined a wall and an old-fashioned cream stove stood in a brick alcove. The room smelt of freshly cooked cake.

Ian and Anna sat down while Mary switched on the electric jug and got out the bottle of lemonade from the fridge. She cut the sponge cake into slices and put them on plates.

'I've got cold lamb for tonight's tea,' she said, 'and I'll make a salad. The tomatoes have been fantastic this year.'

Anna ate her slice of cake and gulped her lemonade. 'Grandma, can I have a rabbit at your place?'

'I don't think it's a good idea, love. Lucky would probably kill it,' Mary said.

Lucky, the old stray cat with a tattered ear who'd wandered in one day and stayed.

Anna's face dropped.

'Why don't you go and see if you can find him?' Mary said.

When Anna had gone, Mary poured Ian another cup of tea and gave him more cake.

'Where's Elaine?' she asked.

'We split up,' Ian said.

'I'm sorry to hear that,' Mary said.

'She wanted to get married.'

Mary put her cup down in its saucer. 'Elaine's not temperamental like Ange. If you got married, she'd make you happy.'

Ian stared at her in surprise. A Catholic, she had been mortified when he and Ange divorced.

Mary gave an embarrassed little cough. 'I know I went on about the divorce as if it was the end of the world, but you shouldn't have to pay for what you did by never having another chance at happiness. It would be nice for Anna to have a little brother or sister.'

Ian swallowed the last of his tea. 'I don't want to marry or have more kids.'

Mary gave him a steady look. 'Don't bite off your nose to spite your face, love. Just because you made a mistake with Ange doesn't mean you'd make one with someone else.'

Ian said nothing. His mum was kind, and only wanted the best for him, but it was her version of best, not his.

Chapter Three

Ian hooked a nervous finger into the collar of his pale blue shirt as the number 67 tram rattled along St Kilda Road towards the city. He was starting his new job at Douglas Lang & Co at the top end of Collins Street, and first impressions counted. His dark hair was neatly cut and his grey suit fresh from the dry cleaners.

His last job had been in a dusty South Melbourne office next to a plumbing supply showroom. He'd shared the space with Lil, who spent half the day on the phone to her mates and the other half complaining about her husband, who spent most of his money at the Moonee Valley racetrack. One Saturday, when Ian felt particularly gloomy about spending another week in the office with Lil, he bought *The Age*, and found an advertisement for a senior accounts clerk at Douglas Lang and Co. He'd been interviewed by Mal Cleary and been offered the job a few days later. The money was quite good, and he needed every penny he could get. Ange was bleeding him dry.

He got off the tram at Collins Street and began walking uphill under the spreading branches of the plane trees. Expensive men's clothes were displayed in one of the windows of George's, but Ian looked straight ahead. When he reached Coates Building, he noticed a cafe on the ground floor and a sandwich bar next door. Across the road stood the Oriental Hotel. He'd be able to grab a quick beer after work, but only a couple. He had no intention of ending up like his father. The tip of Ian's nose itched. He gave it a quick rub with the back of his hand as he entered the building.

...

Jo walked up Collins Street with her head down. When she was little, Maureen said that if she stepped on a crack in the pavement, it would open wide as a crocodile's mouth and swallow her up. Even though Jo knew it was ridiculous, she still felt uneasy if she stepped on one.

At work she checked herself in the mirror and rolled on more mascara. When she went into the main office, she spotted Mr Cleary and a young man she didn't know talking to Mr O'Shaughnessy in his cubicle. Jo sat at her desk and began opening invoices. A few minutes later she heard footsteps coming towards her. She looked up as Mr Cleary said, 'Jo, this is Ian, our new senior accounts clerk.'

Jo's eyes widened. Ian's blue shirt matched his eyes, which held a glint of amusement. Her heart turned over.

'Hello Jo,' he said.

His voice wrapped around her.

Her face warmed. 'Hello.'

Ian and Mr Cleary walked away. She stared after them. Ian moved confidently, as if he knew how good-looking he was. His dark hair lay on his neck, browned by the sun. Reluctantly she turned back to her invoices. In less than a minute, her life had changed. The boring office had become the most exciting place on earth, the old-fashioned desks and battered chairs brave survivors of the past. Typewriters clattered, phones rang and Judith's loud voice boomed from the switchboard in a satisfying combination of sounds. Even Nola, busily typing, looked attractive, the bow on her blouse nicely tied at her throat. But best and most startling of all, was the fact that Robert no longer mattered.

...

After work, Ian caught the tram back to Elwood. His first day had gone well. Mal Cleary and Pat O'Shaughnessy seemed to be decent people, and he had his own cubicle. It was better that way. The office was full of women, and some were good-lookers, but the stand-out was Jo with her short skirt and long legs, sexy bottom lip and eyes that told him exactly what she was thinking. Jo liked him, but he'd steer clear. She was too young.

...

On Saturday, Jo sat at the kitchen table smoking. The rest of the day stretched ahead, as empty as the Nullarbor. She wondered what Ian was doing, and with whom. The thought plunged her into gloom. Over the past week, she'd watched him laughing and joking with Susie, who despite being newly married was a bit flirtatious, and making the odd remark to Judith, but he'd said nothing to her or Ruth. Maybe he thought they were kids, not worth talking to.

Kathleen strolled into the kitchen wearing a pair of shorts and a sleeveless top. 'I'm going to the pool. Why don't you come?'

'Alright.' Jo stubbed out her cigarette and went into her bedroom, undressed and put on her pink gingham bikini. In the mirror her scars were as dark as ever. She scowled. The doctor said they'd fade to a nice, silvery pink, but so far they'd done nothing.

'Hurry up,' Kathleen said from the doorway.

Jo pulled on her shorts and top and shoved a towel, packet of cigarettes and her purse into a canvas beach bag.

They left the house and walked through the housing estate. Sprinklers flicked water onto parched lawns and leaves on the trees hung limp in the heat.

A beat-up Valiant drove past. Its driver tooted and waved. Jo ignored him. Ever since she was twelve boys had tooted, waved or wolf-whistled whenever she walked down the street. At first, she'd been embarrassed. Now she was used to it.

Kathleen watched the car as it roared up the street. 'Idiot. How's the job going?'

'Good,' Jo said. She'd been a fast learner, wanting to impress Mr Cleary, but he wasn't one to give compliments.

'Why don't you go to night school?' Kathleen said. 'You could become an accountant.'

Jo shook her head. 'I don't think so.'

'Because you want to get married and have babies like Miss Goody Two-Shoes. You were so obsessed with Robert, I thought it was gonna be him. The problem is you're aimless. You should set some goals.'

Jo glanced at Kathleen. She was pretty, but she'd never had a boyfriend. If she had, she'd find out there was more to life than school and study.

'I just want to take life as it comes,' Jo said.

Kathleen made a snorting noise. 'You mean hang around waiting for the next boy to ask you out.'

Jo glared at her. 'Not everyone wants to be like you. Working all day and half the night so you can get a scholarship to uni.'

'I'd rather die than not get into uni,' Kathleen said. 'The thing is, you've been given a promotion, and you should make the most of it. You do have brains, you know.'

Jo tossed a length of hair over her shoulder. 'Don't be so patronising.'

'It's a compliment.'

'Fine.'

They walked past the tech school and the service station, where Jo spotted Michael and waved.

'Poor Michael,' Kathleen said. 'The wedding's going to be huge, and he'd rather have a barbeque in the backyard.'

Jo made a face. 'Poor us, having to be bridesmaids.'

'I would have said no,' Kathleen said. 'But I didn't want to leave you in the lurch.'

Jo grinned at her. 'Thanks, sis.'

They passed the row of shops and reached the railway crossing. Noble Park swimming pool lay on the other side of the line, a rectangle of turquoise in dried-out grass. When they arrived, they spread their towels and Kathleen undressed. She was bigger boned than Jo, with the same pale skin, lightly freckled on her nose and shoulders. She walked over to the pool and dived in with a neat splash. When she surfaced, she called, 'Come on, it's lovely.'

'In a minute,' Jo said. She kept her top on and took off her shorts before she walked towards the pool and slid into the cool water, relishing its touch on her hot skin. Her thoughts returned to Ian. She ached to be in his arms. Her pulse raced. She was sure that he knew.

...

'I want to go to the beach,' Anna said. 'Please, Dad.'

Her face wore a pleading look that Ian found irresistible. 'Alright, go put your bathers on.'

Anna rushed into her bedroom.

He went into his own bedroom and put on his bathers. He'd barely pulled them on before she appeared in the doorway wearing a pink and white sundress.

'Are you ready?' she asked impatiently.

He grinned. 'Where's your towel?'

Dismayed, she put a hand to her mouth. 'I forgot.'

'In the bathroom,' he said. 'You don't have to be Miss Perfect all the time.'

'Yes, I do.'

'Yours is the pink one,' he said, and laughed when she looked disgusted.

He packed a bag containing sun lotion, Anna's bucket and spade, and his own towel.

They walked to Elwood Beach under a cloudless sky. Heat bounced off the pavement. The beach was packed with people, their bodies glistening with suntan lotion. Children's shouts filled the air and swimmers bobbed in the sea. Ian found a spot near the water and spread their towels on the sand while Anna took off her sundress and sandals and ran towards the water. He saw her stop, and look down, staring at her foot. He hurried over to her.

'I'm bleeding,' Anna said.

Ian knelt and stared at the wound. She'd been cut by something sharp, but the cut looked shallow.

'It needs a bandaid,' Anna said.

Ian shook his head. 'It's better left open. Let the seawater wash it clean.' He held out his hand. 'Come on, we'll go into the water together.'

Anna gave him a doubtful stare. 'Mum says you have to put bandaids on cuts, or you might get an infection.'

'We'll put a bandaid on it when we get home,' he said. 'Come on.'

A few minutes later, Anna wanted to get out of the water. Ian lay on his towel, watching her build a sandcastle with a moat. The sandcastle was on wet sand, but the tide hadn't reached it. She had to take her bucket to the water to fill the moat.

A couple of girls walked past, both wearing bikinis. They were teenagers, and one of them looked remarkably like Jo. The girl had the same slim build and pale skin, the same dark hair that finished just above her shoulder blades. If she knew he was watching she gave no sign. He wondered what Jo was doing, and who she was with, and felt a fleeting sense of regret that he was no longer a teenager.

Ian looked at Anna again. She was decorating her sandcastle with shells, all of them the same size, placing them in a neat row along the base. Just then a little boy ran up and kicked it a couple of times.

The sandcastle collapsed into a heap of damp sand. Anna's mouth opened in a wail. 'Stop it!'

The little boy ran away. Anna jumped up and ran after him.

'Anna. Stop.'

Anna turned, her face furious.

'Come back,' Ian said.

Anna stomped towards him, then stopped, her eyes on the sand.

'Why were you running after him?' Ian asked.

Anna pouted. 'I wanted to tell him off.'

'You were going to hit him.'

Anna shrugged. 'He deserved it.'

Ian sighed. 'I know it's hard when other kids do the wrong thing, but that little boy was much younger than you.'

Anna's bottom lip stuck out. 'You're saying that 'cause he's a boy.'

'No, I'm not. If he'd been a girl, I'd have said the same thing.' Ian ran a finger lightly down her neck and began to tickle her. She doubled up, laughing. He caught her hand. 'Let's go and get an ice cream.'

Chapter Four

Jo sat at her desk eating a tuna and tomato sandwich. She watched Ian put down his pen and stretch, his suit jacket falling open. Underneath, he wore a pale blue shirt. She wondered if he wore a vest and if he had a hairy chest. He saw her looking at him and smiled. She felt as if an invisible thread connected them, in which each was aware of the other. Maybe it was wishful thinking. She glanced back to *The Post*'s giant crossword. A couple of minutes later she heard footsteps and gulped the last of her sandwich.

'How's it going?' Ian asked.

She looked up. He had an amused glint in his eyes that suggested he knew what she'd been thinking. Her face warmed. 'Good, except for this one.' She pointed at the last unfilled line in the crossword. 'I can't think of his name, the man who invented phones. Four letters.' As Ian bent over the crossword, she caught the clean smell of his aftershave. 'Bell.'

His lips were close to her ear. The heat in her face spread into her neck. 'Thanks.'

As he walked off, she gazed after him. What would he look like undressed? She shouldn't be thinking stuff like this. Folding the copy of *The Post*, she dumped it in her rubbish bin and lit a cigarette.

Two mornings ago, Susie from the typing pool, five-feet tall, wearing six-inch heels and a black miniskirt, had come into the office, her pert face brimming with a secret. She sat down at her desk and beckoned Jo over.

'I was with Jim at the Oriental last night,' Susie said. 'Who do you think was there?

Jo shrugged. 'Don't know.'

'Ian,' Susie said, as if she'd pulled a rabbit out of a hat. 'He was by himself, and we had a couple of drinks. And guess what? He told us he's divorced, and he's got a seven-year-old daughter.'

Jo's eyes rounded. It put Ian in the dangerous category, which made him irresistible.

'I know he's good-looking,' Susie said, 'but he's twenty-eight and he's got a past. I've seen the way you look at him. If you've got any sense, you won't get involved.'

Jo said nothing. It was already too late. She'd fallen in love with him.

...

Ian returned to his cubicle feeling the glow that came from flirting with Jo. Today she wore her navy miniskirt. He imagined putting a hand on her leg just under the hem, feeling the firmness of her thigh. He reminded himself she was only eighteen.

Looking for a diversion, he jerked open his top drawer. Paul had left a half-eaten tube of mints there. As Ian crunched on a mint, he tried to think about the next weekend he was having Anna. They were going to the ice rink at St Kilda. Ange would never take Anna there in a fit, afraid she'd break an ankle, but Ian wanted his daughter to try new things and gain more confidence. He remembered the first time he'd jumped off the high board at the swimming pool, leaping out into space until he hit the water, plunging deep. He'd felt a huge rush of elation that made him want to do it again. Life wasn't worth living unless you were prepared to take a few chances.

Across the office, Ruth and Jo were having a giggly conversation. It was probably about him because they kept shooting looks in his direction. Pleased, he put a hand on his tie to check the knot.

...

The following Monday Jo picked up her purse to go downstairs to the sandwich bar. As she walked past Ian's cubicle he sang out, 'A couple of sausage rolls, please.'

She stepped inside the cubicle, taking the note he offered without touching his fingers. 'With sauce?'

'Thanks,' he said, smiling. 'I missed breakfast this morning.'

Jo pushed the note into her purse. As she went out, she felt his eyes on her legs. How long would it be before he asked her out? If he didn't do it soon, she'd die.

Waiting for the lift, she spun her usual fantasy in which she and Ian were in the office after everyone had gone home. She imagined him coming over to her desk, bending down to kiss her. He'd take her hand and lead her to the chief executive's office where a huge, polished table in dark red wood stood in the middle of the room. They'd make love on the table while trams rattled along Collins Street far below. It would be exciting making love in that place where old men in expensive suits met to talk about business.

Downstairs at the sandwich bar she bought two paper bags of sausage rolls and sauce, so hot they almost burned her fingers, and took them upstairs. Ian's hand brushed hers as she handed him a bag. She felt a flicker of heat.

'How was your weekend?' he asked.

Surprised, she said, 'Alright.'

'I bet you went out with your boyfriend.'

She shook her head. 'We split. I went to a party.'

He smiled. 'Naturally.'

She made a face. 'It was a family party.'

The party had been held at Uncle Sean's, one of her dad's brothers. Mum's sister Auntie Eileen had got drunk and sang 'Danny Boy' in a voice that cracked on the high notes and struggled to find the lows while Maureen and Michael did their happy couple act and Kathleen, looking gloomy, checked out the small bookcase of paperbacks. Mum gossiped with the wives of her brothers – she didn't like some of them, but they wouldn't know it – and the men stood nursing glasses of beer and talking about cars, the cricket and the weather.

As parties went, it could have been worse. Jo had been to some where the boys got drunk around the niner, and the girls were left to look after themselves. Sometimes someone would go outside and spew, or a girl and a boy would disappear for a while. Jo always smoked so much that her throat felt raw, and usually she let a boy take her home and kiss her on the front porch. In the morning, she'd wake up feeling not exactly dirty, but less clean.

'I don't really like parties,' she said.

Ian lifted his eyebrows. 'What *do* you like?'

The smell of his aftershave, the thrill of opening the first page of a new library book, old buildings, the miniature worlds of rock pools. But she wouldn't tell Ian about those. 'Dancing,' she said.

'Gogo dancing?'

She shook her head.

'Ballroom?'

'Too old-fashioned.' She could have cut her tongue out. Maybe he liked ballroom dancing.

He smiled. 'What kind of dancing, then?'

'The twist.' She held up her bag of sausage rolls. 'I'd better eat these.'

'Go ahead.'

Red-faced, she made her escape.

...

Ian bit into a sausage roll. He felt elated that Jo had no boyfriend, but there were ten years between them, and it showed. When he overheard Jo and Ruth talking it was about clothes, and shoes, and going out, and which pop group was coming to Festival Hall. Sometimes Jo mentioned the names Maureen and Kathleen, which he guessed were her sisters. If Jo mentioned her mother, she pulled a face. He wondered if he and Jo spent a few hours together whether she'd bore him stupid. Maybe she'd be bored stupid by him. He didn't have a clue who was in the Top Ten and he preferred women without their clothes on. He'd imagined Jo naked in his bed quite a few times. She seemed unaware of how sexy she was. He guessed she might have had some experience with one or two boys, but never a man.

Ian swallowed his sausage roll. If he did decide to ask Jo out, it wouldn't be straight forward. The people at work would find out, and after it was over they'd side with Jo, while he'd be seen as the bastard who'd taken advantage of her. Normally, he didn't care what people thought, but he liked working here. He glanced over at Jo. She'd finished eating her sausage rolls and sat smoking, a faraway look on her face. He wondered what she was thinking.

...

Jo stared out of the window. Puffy clouds floated across the sky. She was getting desperate. Was Ian really interested in her? He flirted with Susie, although she seemed to be the one who started it, and Judith, who'd told the girls in a quiet voice that he could put his shoes under her bed any day. Judith and her husband were trying for a baby. She said when they had sex she avoided going to the toilet for a bit, so she wouldn't lose any of her husband's sperm. Last year she had a stillborn baby boy at six months. She'd called him Jacob Ernest. Jo couldn't imagine how awful it would be having a dead baby. Hopefully it wouldn't happen to her.

Chapter Five

May came with cool nights and misty mornings, falling leaves of russet and gold. As Jo clattered towards the station one morning she wondered if Ian would ever ask her out. It had been almost three months since he'd started working at Douglas Lang. Surely, he knew how she felt.

Most weekends she stayed at home playing records like 'Unchained Melody', or 'I Will Follow Him'. She knew she was wallowing in misery but felt unable to stop. Other times she walked Rufus or lay on her bed reading books she borrowed from the Athenaeum Library – *Justine*, and *Melissa*, and for a change, *Animal Farm*, where she shed tears over the old horse. A couple of times she went to the Springvale dance but came home alone. To make things worse, Maureen was on her case about John, who worked with Michael at the garage.

'He gets that sheepy look on his face whenever he sees you,' Maureen said. 'Why don't I organise a foursome?'

Jo shook her head. 'No thanks.'

Maureen stared at her. 'Are you interested in someone?'

'No.'

'You're lying,' Maureen said. 'You've been playing too many sad records. You can't hide it from me forever.'

Jo shrugged. 'I told you before. There's no-one.'

...

When Jo arrived at work, Ian sat in his cubicle looking at a spreadsheet. She hung up her raincoat and checked herself in the mirror. Clean hair, no spots. She brushed on more mascara and walked out into the office. Ian looked up. Jo's heart seemed to miss a beat as she walked towards her desk. Sitting down, she lit a cigarette, tossed the packet into the petty cash tin and locked it. Ian pointed at the petty cash tin and raised his eyebrows. She made a ball shape with her hands, getting smaller. *Cutting down*. He smiled.

...

Ian turned back to his spreadsheet. The way Jo moved reminded him of a cat. She was irresistible. He wondered what it would feel like to have his mouth over her full bottom lip, while his hand slipped under her tight pink jumper and found her small breasts. Ian sighed. Hopefully his attraction to Jo would subside, but right now it was showing no signs of it.

...

After work, Jo walked with Ruth down Collins Street. Late afternoon sunlight filtered through the leaves of the plane trees onto the pavement.

'I reckon he's gonna ask you out soon,' Ruth said. 'He looks at you all the time.'

Jo made a face. 'I wish he would. I'm going out of my mind.'

'Maybe he's worried 'cause he's a lot older.'

They stopped at the traffic lights; Ruth pressed the button.

'I heard him telling Moira he's going to the St Kilda ice rink on Saturday afternoon,' Ruth said.

Moira, in her forties, the mother hen of the office, also rumoured to be a spy for management.

'Why don't we go?' Ruth said.

Jo's pulse raced. If they met at the rink he'd have the perfect opportunity. *But what if he's not interested?* She batted the thought away. 'Yes. Let's.'

...

On Saturday morning Jo woke early. Immediately she felt tense. Would this be the magical day when Ian asked her out, or would she come home in the depths of despair? She slid out of bed, pulled on her pink dressing gown and wandered into the bathroom. As she turned on the shower, she heard Mum's footsteps going past the bathroom door. There'd be no mention of St Kilda. Mum thought St Kilda was a place of drunks and hobos, and girls weren't safe there.

That afternoon Jo arrived in St Kilda and waited outside the ice rink, a daggy old building on the Esplanade. A cold wind blew in from the bay, making her shiver.

Ruth appeared, rugged up in her duffle coat, cheeks pink and slightly out of breath.

They went into the musty smelling lobby, paid the entry fee, hired their skates and walked into the rink. Bone-chilling cold rose from the ice, and old-fashioned dance music boomed from the speakers. Rows of seats covered with threadbare plush surrounded the rink. Jo sat down and laced up her skates, then she and Ruth went out onto the ice. Jo found it hard to stay upright, so she kept close to the rail at the edge.

'Hey girls.'

Jo looked across the ice and spotted Ian skating towards them. He was smiling and holding the hand of a little girl about six or seven, buttoned up in a blue coat. Her breath caught. *Oh My God, he's with his daughter.*

Ian and the little girl came to a stop in front of them. 'This is a surprise,' Ian said. 'I didn't know you two skated.'

Jo's face burned. 'This is our first time.'

'Jo and Ruth, this is Anna, my daughter.'

He was obviously proud of her.

Anna was quite tall, with long thin legs. Masses of dark wavy hair fell to her shoulders and her face was the same shape as Ian's, with a wide brow and jaw. She was beautiful.

'How about Anna and me teach you two how to skate?' Ian said.

He held his hand out to Jo, and she took it. Her hand tingled, as if an electric current had passed between them. Maybe he felt it too because his hand tightened around hers. Close up, she was aware of the tang of his aftershave. She hoped he could smell Maureen's expensive perfume that she'd sprayed under her ears.

'We'll go around the edge first,' Ian said, 'so you girls can get the hang of it. Anna, are you holding Ruth's hand?'

Anna made a face. 'Yes, dad.'

They all laughed.

The four of them slowly circled the rink, Jo and Anna on each side of Ian, and Ruth holding Anna's hand. A couple of times Jo almost lost her balance. 'I'm no good,' she said.

Ian squeezed her hand. 'Relax, you just need practice.'

She wondered what it would feel like to be in his arms.

'Daddy, I'm thirsty,' Anna said. 'Can I have a Coke?'

Ian looked at Jo and Ruth. 'Do you girls want a drink?'

'A Coke, please,' Jo said.

'Yes, a Coke,' Ruth echoed.

'I'll sit down for a bit,' Jo said.

Ruth gave Jo a look. *Here's your chance.* She held out her hand to Anna. 'Shall we go round the edge? We can hold onto the rail.'

Anna looked up at Ian, her face doubtful.

'Try it,' he said.

Ian went off to buy the Cokes while Jo sat and watched Ruth and Anna moving slowly around the rink. Her stomach felt tight with anxiety. Was he going to ask her out, or not? If he was, he had to do it soon.

A few minutes later Ian appeared, holding four bottles of Coke.

Their fingers touched as he handed Jo a bottle, its sides beaded with moisture.

'Thanks,' she said, unscrewing the cap and gulping down some Coke. Her eyes watered and she sneezed. *Damn.* So much for looking poised.

'I thought you'd be out there pirouetting on the ice.'

There was a smile in his voice.

'Bulldust. You know I can barely stand up,' she said.

She'd unbuttoned her coat. He was looking down at her breasts in her tight pink jumper, and the zip on her boys' jeans. 'How about we have a drink after work some time?' he asked.

Her heart leapt. 'I'd like that.'

'What about next Wednesday, at the Australia hotel. Do you know where it is?'

'Yes,' she said. 'Collins Street.'

'I'd prefer it if the people at work didn't know,' he said. 'Will Ruth keep quiet?'

'Yes,' she repeated.

'Are you a yes girl?' he teased.

'Only with you.' Her face burned. She'd been too forward.

He smiled. 'Good.'

She looked away. The music seemed louder in her ears and the rink gleamed pale and cold. Ian sat down in the seat next to her. His after-shave was the sexiest smell in the world. He waved to Anna and Ruth, and they came over.

Later, on their way to the tram, Ruth said, 'He's asked you out, hasn't he?'

Jo smiled. 'Yes, but please don't say anything at work. We want to keep it to ourselves for a while.'

'Everyone will guess,' Ruth said. 'You wait and see.'

...

When Jo got home, the house was warm and smelt of Saturday night's tea – sausages, mash and fried onions. The six o'clock news on Channel 10 blared from the living room. Rufus charged down the hall. Jo fondled his ears. 'I'm home,' she yelled. No-one answered. She felt a momentary pang. If she left tomorrow no-one would notice.

She went into the bedroom and stared into the mirror. Her eyes shone. She felt like shouting her news to the world, but she'd keep quiet. Mum would ask if he was a Catholic and Maureen would nag her to find out more. She'd called Robert a loser (she'd been right about that) and Tony, Jo's previous boyfriend, peculiar because he smoked a pipe. Maureen said nothing about Kathleen's weird friend Gary, who'd painted his bedroom walls black and given her one of his paintings, a mess of red, purple, black and white, other than saying she wouldn't put that ugly thing in her house even if she was paid. Kathleen had laughed at her. 'It shows you've got no taste,' she'd said. Kathleen knew exactly what to say to Maureen, but Jo only thought of something later. It was irritating.

She hung her coat up in the wardrobe. Today she'd seen Ian as a dad. He was kind and loving towards Anna, giving her lots of attention. When

Anna fell on the ice, he held out his hand to help her up. 'You don't quit,' he said. 'Jo and Ruth aren't quitting, are they?'

When Jo fell, the ice felt hard and it hurt, but Ian helped her up and she kept skating. Ruth found it easier to keep her balance and soon began to look quite graceful. Jo felt clumsy and useless, but it didn't matter. Ian had asked her out, and she felt as light as air.

...

Ian and Anna caught the tram back to Elwood, ate hamburgers and chips at a café and went home to his flat. He turned on the shower for Anna and left before she'd taken her clothes off. His solicitor had told him to be careful when Anna came on access visits. Quite a few men had been accused by their ex-wives of touching up their kids. When Anna came out of the bathroom in her pyjamas he rubbed her hair with a towel and gave her a wide-toothed comb. After she'd combed her hair, they watched TV together and Anna cuddled into him on the couch, warm as a puppy, smelling of clean hair and skin.

Ian had no idea what they watched. He was thinking what a coincidence it had been meeting Jo and Ruth at the rink, and how sexy Jo had looked in her jeans and tight jumper. There'd been a zip at the front of the jeans. Looking at it, he'd imagined pulling it down and slipping his hand inside. He'd given into the impulse to ask her out. It was a risk, but he'd try not to think of the difference in their ages. She wasn't a schoolgirl. He'd asked Jo to keep quiet about their relationship, but the women at work would soon find out. They seemed to have a sixth sense for these things. Hopefully, when it ended, he and Jo could be nice to each other.

Ian's neck ached; he rolled his head around to ease the tension. Asking Jo out was the most exciting thing he'd done in ages, but it came with risks. He'd try and ignore them.

Chapter Six

On Wednesday after work Jo got off the tram at the Australia hotel and saw Ian waiting outside. Her pulse raced. He took her arm as they went through the hotel door, guiding her upstairs into the lounge, where the roar of voices rose to the ceiling. People sat around tables, eating and drinking, and the air smelt of beer and cigarette smoke. They sat at a small table marked with wet rings. Jo perched on the edge of her seat. She hoped she wouldn't say or do anything stupid.

'Would you like some oysters?' Ian asked.

Jo shook her head. Horrible slimy things that slid down your throat. 'No thanks.' She wondered if it was obvious they were on their first date.

'How about a Brandy Crusta?'

She had no idea what it was. 'Yes, please.'

Ian went up to the bar while Jo unbuttoned her coat. Pulling out her cigarettes, she lit up. Her hand shook as she held the match.

Ian returned with the drinks. Hers had sugar pressed into the rim of the glass and a twist of lemon peel. His looked like red wine. He handed her the drink and sat down, loosening his tie. 'So, how do you like your job?'

'It's more interesting than my last one,' she said. 'Do you like yours?'

He shrugged. 'It pays the bills.' He leaned towards her. 'I thought it would be nice if we got to know each other outside the office.'

She gulped some of her Brandy Crusta. There wasn't much to know other than that she had scars on her body and had fallen in love with him.

'You don't like parties but you like dancing,' he said. 'What else?

'Going to the movies.'

'Did you like *The Sound of Music*?'

She made a face. 'No, James Bond.'

'Have you seen *Thunderball*?'

She nodded. 'Of course.'

'I haven't seen it.'

'I'd be happy to go again.'

He put a hand over hers. 'I'm sure you would.'

She felt a surge of warmth.

'I'm guessing you like pop music,' he said.

'Yes, The Beatles and The Stones. The Righteous Brothers. Dusty Springfield.' She looked into his eyes. 'You haven't told me anything about you.'

He smiled. 'You already know. I'm divorced and I have a seven-year-old daughter.'

'What else?'

He turned over her hand, made a circle on her palm with his index finger. 'I'm attracted to you, but I'm twenty-eight and you're eighteen. That's a big gap.'

'I don't care,' she said.

He smiled. 'I'm not looking for anything serious, just to have fun. What about you?'

She stared at him over the rim of her glass. He wanted her for as long as it suited him. She felt an emptiness that might be grief. But what if he fell in love with her? Wouldn't he change his mind?

He was watching her closely. She'd say whatever he wanted. 'I want to have fun,' she said. An awful thought struck her. 'Does that mean you'll go out with other women?'

'No,' he said. 'I'm a one-woman man.' He leaned closer. 'It wouldn't be fair to stop you from seeing other people. You might find someone you'll want to get serious with.'

She was appalled. 'I don't want to see anyone else.'

His eyebrows lifted. 'Are you sure? You can change your mind whenever you like.'

She tilted her glass to her lips. 'I'm sure.'

'Don't drink it too fast,' he warned. 'I don't want to get you drunk.' He touched her glass with his. 'To us.'

'To us,' she echoed. She'd made a commitment, even if he hadn't.

After a couple more drinks, they left the hotel. Jo felt a little drunk.

'We should eat,' Ian said. 'Where do you want to go?'

'Chinatown.' It was her favourite place, dark and shabby, with secret alleys and silent buildings, their old doors hung with posters printed in Chinese characters.

'Which place?'

'You choose,' she said.

'Alright,' he said. 'I'll take you to my favourite. It doesn't look much from the outside, but the food is fantastic.'

They left the hotel and walked up Collins Street. He slipped an arm around her waist, and she leaned into him.

'I'm glad you agreed,' he said.

'I'm glad too.' The alcohol had made her feel bold. She giggled and waggled a finger at him. 'I bet there's a question you're dying to ask but you don't think you can.'

'What's that?'

'If I'm a virgin.'

'Are you?' he said in a light voice.

'No,' she said. 'I had a boyfriend I thought I loved.'

'Good,' Ian said. 'I don't want to feel responsible for deflowering you.'

She giggled again. 'Deflowering? What kind of a word is that?'

Ian grinned, a flash of white in the gloom. 'I remember it from English class at school.'

She liked that he remembered a word like that. Maybe he read books.

They turned the corner into Swanston Street. The city was almost empty. A couple of winos slumped in doorways and a solitary tram rumbled past.

'Where do you live?' Ian asked.

'Noble Park. It's near Dandenong.'

'That's a long way out.'

'It takes forty-five minutes to get to the city,' Jo said. 'Where do you live?'

'I've got a flat in Elwood.'

'Do you share with anyone?'

He shook his head. 'I live by myself.'

The thought of him having his own place thrilled her. Soon, they'd make love in his bed.

They turned into Little Bourke Street and went past David Wang's emporium. At the mouth of an alley, they stopped and kissed. His tongue probed her mouth. She pulled him closer. Her body tingled. They drew apart and hand in hand walked up the street to a tiny cafe, dimly lit. Inside, next to a wooden staircase, four old Chinese men sat at a table. They were playing a game with dice and white pieces marked with Chinese characters.

'What are they playing?' Jo asked, as they climbed the stairs.

'Mahjong,' Ian said.

She'd never heard of it.

At the top of the stairs was a small room lit with red lanterns, and the air smelt of spices. Chinese people sat at tables scattered around the room. There were no Europeans.

They sat at a table for two against the wall. Ian's hand rested on Jo's thigh. She felt a flicker of heat.

A waiter emerged from a door and came over.

Jo looked at the menu, undecided.

'Would you like me to order?' Ian asked.

She nodded.

When the food arrived, rice steamed in a blue and white china bowl, and there were several large platters. Ian poured her a cup of straw-coloured tea. 'We'll share,' he said. 'That way you get to try different dishes.'

Jo ate from every platter. Vegetables crunched in her mouth along with tender morsels of prawn and chicken in spicy sauces, and perfectly cooked rice.

'This is fab,' she said, between mouthfuls.

Ian grinned. 'It is.'

Afterwards, they caught the tram to Elwood and Ian's block of flats, but instead of going inside, Ian led her to his car, a grey Holden, parked close to the fence. She felt vaguely disappointed.

They got in. The car smelt of recently cleaned vinyl. Trying to ignore the smell, she sat close to him, a hand on his leg.

Ian started the motor and drove out into the street. 'Are you any good at reading maps?' he asked.

'Not bad,' she said.

'There's a Melway on the back seat. Tell me how to get to Noble Park.' He switched on the overhead light.

Jo reached over her seat to get the Melway and flipped through the index at the back. Looking at books in moving cars made her feel queasy. She turned to the front so she could see the major roads. The page swam under her gaze. She swallowed, focusing on the page. The smell of recently cleaned vinyl filled her nose. She was going to be sick. 'Stop the car,' she said.

Ian pulled into the kerb. Jo flung open her door and spewed into the gutter. She felt Ian's hands holding back her hair. *Oh God.*

She gave one last spasm then sat up, opening her handbag for her hankie. Wiping her face, she said, 'Sorry,' in a low voice.

'Are you feeling better?' he asked.

'Yes.' She shoved the hankie into her handbag and scrabbled around for her perfume, spraying it under her ears.

Ian bent over and picked up the Melway, which had slid off her lap onto the floor. He went through the pages until he found the right ones, looked at them, and tossed the Melway into the back.

'Do you have any lollies?' she asked.

'No,' he said. 'We'll stop at the next service station.'

Ian started the car and drove into the traffic. An ambulance screamed past. Ten minutes later, a cop flagged them to slow down, joining a line of cars driving slowly past a huddle of people. Cop cars with flashing blue lights and several ambulances were parked on the side of the road. Two cars, both smashed in at the front, stood at the kerb.

'A head on,' Ian said. 'It looks bad. You should make the most of life before it's too late.'

She wondered if he'd known and loved people who'd died, but she didn't dare ask. The only person she'd known who'd died had been her grandmother on her mum's side, and she'd been very sick.

They stopped at a service station where Jo darted to the toilets and stared at her stricken face in the mirror. He'd spent money buying her a lovely meal and she'd spewed it up into the gutter. He'd never ask her out again. Turning on the cold tap she rinsed her mouth then added some hot water to bathe her face. When she went back to the car, Ian handed her a bottle of Coke and a packet of mints.

He drove towards Noble Park, while Jo swigged Coke and crunched on mints. Her throat ached. 'I'm so sorry,' she said.

He gave her a quick glance. 'It's not a big deal. I shouldn't have bought you those Brandy Crustas.'

He sat relaxed, hands resting on the steering wheel. If he dumped her, she'd never forgive herself.

They reached her house and he pulled into the kerb, turning off the lights. She glanced at the house with its darkened windows. Everyone was in bed.

They went along the path. High above, stars glittered. On the porch, she caught a faint smell of roses, the last of the season. They stopped by the front door.

He put a hand on her shoulder and squeezed it. 'See you tomorrow,' he said.

…

Ian got into his car, started the motor and drove up the street. The car smelt faintly of vomit. He wound down the window and the cold night air rushed in, blowing his hair about. He felt about eighteen.

…

'Turn it off,' Maureen grumbled.

Jo turned off the alarm as the memory of last night's disaster flooded her mind. She burned with shame. How could she forget him holding back her hair while she spewed in the gutter? He'd dump her for sure. She shed a few wretched tears into her pillow. Maybe she should call in sick today? No, better to go in and face him. She threw back the covers. The room felt icy, and her stomach growled with hunger.

In the kitchen, Monica sat at the yellow formica table buttering a piece of toast. 'You were late last night.'

Jo got out the packet of Corn Flakes from the cupboard. 'I worked back and didn't notice the time.'

Monica frowned. 'You shouldn't have to work so late.'

Jo tipped the Corn Flakes into a bowl, sloshing milk on top. 'We only worked 'til half seven then we went to Chinatown to eat.'

'Who's we?' Monica asked.

'Ruth, me and Ian.' Jo sat down and spooned Corn Flakes into her mouth.

Monica poured tea into her cup. 'I don't like you coming home on the train late at night. It's dangerous.'

'Ian gave me a lift.'

'Does he live near here?'

Jo shrugged. 'I don't know.'

'You don't know very much.'

'Why should I?' Jo said. 'We just work together.' She carried the bowl to the spotless sink. It might be true. She could have killed off their relationship before it had even started.

Chapter Seven

When Jo walked into work, Ian glanced up at her and smiled. She forced herself to smile back. Sitting at her desk, she started opening her mail. Her phone rang. She lifted the receiver.

'How about meeting me downstairs just after one?' Ian said quietly.

'Alright,' she said, and put the receiver down. A wave of panic swept through her. *Did he want them to meet so he could end it?*

At five past one she headed downstairs, stomach churning.

Ian stood outside. She felt a tiny flutter of hope as he grabbed her hand. Dry leaves scrunched under their feet as they walked along Collins Street past the Melbourne Club and turned into Exhibition Street, where the glass tower of the Southern Cross Hotel loomed against the sky.

'Where are we going?' she asked.

'To get souvlaki.'

'What is it?'

'Lamb and salad wrapped in flatbread. It's Greek.'

'I'd love that.'

He glanced down at her. 'You're not scared of trying new foods.'

'No, I like it.'

He squeezed her hand. 'So do I.'

Was he trying to be kind before he dumped her? Tears pricked her eyes. 'About last night,' she said. 'I'm so sorry.'

He shrugged. 'Forget it. How about we go to Luna Park on Saturday night?'

Instantly the day became perfect, like the sun coming out after a storm, with everything washed clean and raindrops glistening on spiders' webs. 'Yes,' she said. 'I'd love to.'

...

Back at Coates Building, Ian insisted on Jo getting into the lift while he took the stairs. Being with her even for a short time made him feel like a teenager again. He climbed the stairs, whistling.

...

Jo opened the front door to the smell of Thursday night's lamb casserole. Maureen sat at the kitchen table poring over a list, a cigarette burning in an ashtray next to her. 'You've got that dreamy-eyed look again,' she said. 'Who's the lucky man?'

'No-one,' Jo said.

Maureen's eyes glinted. 'Don't lie. It's Ian, isn't it?'

There was no point denying it. 'Yes,' Jo said.

'Has he got another girlfriend?'

Jo shook her head. 'No.'

'That's an improvement on Robert. Is he good-looking?'

Jo smiled. 'Very.'

'Where does he live?'

'Elwood.'

'By himself?'

Jo nodded.

'Ooh, your own little love nest. I'm jealous. How come he lives by himself?'

Jo hesitated. 'He's a bit older than me.'

Maureen's eyes narrowed. 'How much?'

'Ten years.'

Maureen's eyes opened wider. 'Ooh, you've got yourself a man. I can't wait to meet him.'

Jo's chest filled with dread. Maureen had a talent for finding out people's secrets.

'I've got to change the guest list,' Maureen said. 'There's been a falling out in Michael's family.'

Shadows lay under her eyes. Were all weddings like this? Lots of planning, things going wrong, people arguing.

'Let me see.'

Maureen pushed the list towards Jo. On their side, there was Auntie Eileen, who was unmarried, and Uncle Seamus, Uncle Pat and Uncle Joe, all married with kids, most of them grown up, who were either married or engaged, or had boyfriends or girlfriends. On Michael's side, his parents, uncles, aunts, cousins and friends. Maureen had scored out Michael's friend Paul and his wife Anne.

'What happened?' Jo asked.

'Michael got Paul a cheap car and it broke down. He blames Michael. But you know Paul; he's touchy.'

'I'll put Ian on the list,' Maureen continued. 'Just in case you're still going out with him.'

Jo felt an emptiness in her chest. By then, she and Ian would have split. 'Alright,' she said.

...

On Saturday morning, Jo woke early. She stretched and wiggled her toes. Tonight, she'd meet Ian at Luna Park. Tonight, they'd make love.

She put on her pink dressing gown and went out to the kitchen, pulling up the blinds. Outside, a rain-soaked garden and heavy sky. Mum would be up soon, and Maureen, who worked at the salon on Saturday mornings. Jo made herself a mug of coffee and lit a cigarette. She heard Maureen's alarm go off, followed by the bathroom door closing and the splash of a shower.

Monica came into the kitchen zipped into her pale blue dressing gown.

'I've boiled the jug,' Jo said.

'Why are you up so early?' Monica asked.

'I'm going to the city.'

'You work there all week. Why on earth do you want to go at the weekend?'

'I'm meeting Ian.'

'Ian from work?'

'Yes,' Jo said.

Monica stared at her. 'Is he Catholic?'

Jo took a last drag and stubbed out her cigarette. 'How should I know?'

'Haven't you asked?'

'No.'

'Where does he live?'

'Elwood.'

'With his family?'

'I don't know.'

Monica frowned. 'How long have you known him?'

'Three months.'

'Three months and you know nothing about him. I don't understand young people today.'

Maureen came in, wearing her black salon clothes. 'Did Jo tell you she's got a new boyfriend?'

'Yes, and she hardly knows a thing about him,' Monica said.

Jo glared at her. 'Give me a break, we haven't been out yet.' *God, I'm a liar.* She got up, went into the bedroom and yanked open her drawer. Yesterday she'd bought a new black bra, trimmed with lace, and matching panties. It was important she looked as sophisticated as possible. She'd take a shower, wash her hair, maybe put on a face pack. No, not the face pack. It might bring out a spot.

...

Ian got out of bed and opened the venetians. Autumn sunlight spilled across the carpet. He padded into the bathroom and stripped off his singlet and underpants. Stepping into the shower he felt a pleasurable sense of anticipation. Tonight, Jo would be in his bed.

...

Jo met Ian outside Luna Park. The night was cold, a full moon in the sky. Ian wore a jacket and pants and a checked shirt. Her pulse raced. He was so handsome.

'You look fantastic,' he said, glancing at her pale blue coat, open to show her dress.

She smiled. 'Thanks.' He put an arm around her as they walked through the open mouth of the moon face into the fairground sounds of screams and music. Brightly lit kiosks and rides glittered in the dark.

'What rides do you want to go on?' he asked.

'The Big Dipper.'

'You like to be scared,' he said.

She giggled. 'I'm going to need protection.'

He grinned. 'I'm your man.'

On the Big Dipper she held her breath as the carriages climbed high above the park, screaming with excitement as they swooped downhill. When she looked at him, he was smiling.

When they got off, he said, 'More scares coming up.'

She cuddled into him on the ghost train as it clanked through cobwebs, past a rubbishy copy of an ancient Egyptian mummy that popped out of the dark. They kissed; he touched her breast inside her unbuttoned coat. She felt as if she might faint.

He was surprised she didn't react to the large black spider that dangled in front of her face.

'Only snakes,' she said, when he asked what scared her.

'What about the Giggle Palace?' he asked when the ghost train stopped.

'No,' she said. 'Those mirrors make you look ugly.'

'You'd never look ugly,' he said. 'What else?'

'The shooting gallery.'

His eyebrows went up. 'Are you telling me you're handy with a gun?'

She smiled, feeling superior. 'Wait and see.'

She won a fluffy blue monkey, and carried it under one arm as they headed towards a food van. He held her hand. She wished time would stand still; the night never end.

'I can't believe how well you shoot,' he said. 'You're a real little Annie Oakley.'

She thought she heard admiration in his voice. 'It's one of my secrets.'

'That sounds interesting.'

'My grandpa belonged to a rifle club. He used to put old soup tins on a log and get me to shoot them.'

'Tell me another one.'

A scarred body, her jealousy of Maureen – mum's pet – who could walk into a room and have everyone think she was the most beautiful girl they'd ever seen. Not those.

'I can't swim very well.'

He slipped an arm around her. 'So, if we go to the beach and you get into trouble, I'll have to be your lifesaver.'

She nodded. 'Yes.'

'What if I can't swim?' he teased.

She looked up at him. 'You can. Very well.'

His arm tightened. 'I might need some encouragement. You could wave your bikini top at me.'

She looked at him from under her lashes. 'Only if no-one else is there.'

'The bottom half would work even better.'

She smiled. 'Dream on.'

'Have you ever swum naked?' he asked.

She was taken aback. 'No. Have you?'

'Yes. Me and my mates were camping at the beach. It felt so free.'

She wondered what it would be like to take her clothes off and not be embarrassed about her scars.

'We should do it,' he said.

'Yes,' she said, but didn't want to.

They queued for jam doughnuts dusted with sugar and drank tea from paper cups. The night had got colder.

'Where now?' he asked.

'The River Caves,' she said.

In the River Caves he put his hand on her thigh under her dress, stroking it with his thumb. 'Let's go to my place.'

'Yes,' she said. She was floating.

They walked towards his car. When they got inside, she put the monkey on the back seat. They kissed, and he put his tongue in her mouth. She touched him through his trousers.

'Not yet,' he groaned.

She kept her hand on his leg as he drove into the traffic, watching the lights of St Kilda slide past. She wished she could stop worrying about him seeing her naked.

Ian's flat was upstairs in a modern block of cream brick. On the small piece of ground in front stood an old tree that had managed to survive the builders. He put his arm around her as they climbed the concrete stairs, fumbled for his keys as they stood together outside his door. When they stepped inside, he switched on the living room light. She saw an old dark red couch, a bookcase full of paperbacks, a sideboard with an expensive-looking record player on top, and a small, kidney-shaped coffee table with no ashtray. Everything looked old, except for the record player. She wondered what books he read; what music he listened to.

'Give me your coat,' he said.

She slipped it off her shoulders and handed it to him, watching as he laid it over the back of the old couch. Then he took off his jacket and held out his hand. She gripped it tightly as they went into the bedroom, bare except for a double bed, made up with striped sheets and checked blankets. He switched on a lamp that stood on a cardboard box.

They lay on the bed, to her the night seemed hushed, waiting. She unbuttoned his shirt and undid the waistband of his trousers, sliding her hand inside. He felt for the zip at the back of her dress and slid it down, then helped her take it off, then her slip, pantyhose and undies. The cold air brought her skin out in goosebumps.

'Here, get in,' he said, pulling back the covers. He watched her as she slid between them. Luckily her scarred side was away from him. When he was ready, she wrapped her legs around him as he rolled on top.

It didn't last long.

'I'm sorry,' he said. 'Next time will be better.' He put his hand between her legs. She gasped.

'Hasn't anyone done this to you before?' he asked.

'No,' she whispered. Her body arched, fell back.

'You're so beautiful,' he said.

She put a hand up to his face. He hadn't met Maureen.

...

On the way to Noble Park Ian said, 'Where do you want to go tomorrow?'

'Williamstown,' she said.

He sounded puzzled. 'What's at Williamstown?'

'Ice cream.'

'In this weather?'

'I'd eat ice cream in a blizzard.'

In the light of a streetlamp, she saw him grin. 'Alright, Williamstown it is.'

'I'll catch the train and meet you at Flinders Street,' she said.

'Are you sure?' he asked. 'I'm happy to come and pick you up.'

'No, it'll be fine.'

At Jo's house, Ian walked her to the front door and kissed her goodnight, whispered 'Sleep well,' and went back to his car. It was a clear night, the sky sparkling with stars. He started the motor and drove out into the street. He knew why Jo had insisted on catching the train. She didn't want her parents to meet him. It was probably for the best. He felt wildly happy.

...

The next day Ian waited for Jo at Flinders Street Station. When she emerged from the barriers and walked towards him, he thought how sexy she looked in her short coat and jeans, her hair loose over her shoulders. Images of her naked body from last night came to his mind. Maybe he should have invited her to the flat instead of agreeing to go to Williamstown, but the idea was so unexpected it had appealed to him.

When they arrived in Williamstown, he bought a couple of Eskimo Pies from a milk bar. 'Let's go for a walk,' he said.

They ambled along the seafront, listening to the roar and suck of the waves. He felt the warmth of her arm tucked inside his.

'I'd have never thought of bringing you here to eat ice cream in this weather,' he said.

She smiled up at him. 'I like being outside.'

'We could be outside at Elwood.'

'But it's so nice here.' She waved an arm at the old stone buildings lining the street. 'Aren't they beautiful?'

He glanced at her in surprise. 'So, you wouldn't approve if they were torn down.'

'I'd be horrified.'

He was surprised, he'd thought she'd only like pop stars and clothes. 'So would I.'

They sat on a bench facing the yachts. The wind was starting to give him earache. 'Have you ever been on a yacht?' he asked.

She shook her head. 'No.'

'I have,' he said. 'It's fun, unless the sea's choppy.'

She made a face. 'No thank you.'

Remembering Wednesday night, he squeezed her hand. 'Probably not. You're looking cold. Shall we go?'

He drove her back to his flat and they went to bed, and this time was better for him. He took his time before he entered her, stroking her naked body and running his tongue around her nipples, which were small and pink. Later he brewed coffee in his Italian coffee pot and poured it into two tiny cups.

'Are you Italian?' she asked.

'No, Ange is. My ex-wife.'

Her expression changed.

He felt annoyed with himself for mentioning Ange.

'Come into the living room,' he said.

She made a beeline for his record collection and flipped through it.

'Do you like any of them?' he asked.

She held up his Elvis Presley album.

'You've got good taste,' he said.

When he drove her home, it was dusk and the lights were on in her house. He leaned forward and kissed her. 'I'll see you to the door.'

She shook her head. 'No, it's alright.'

'Do you think your parents will be lying in wait?' he asked, amused.

'No,' she said. 'See you tomorrow.'

He watched as she opened the door and ran up the path to the house, disappearing inside. He wished she could have stayed with him for longer.

Chapter Eight

On Monday morning, in the girls' room, Susie said, 'You and Ian are going out, aren't you?'

Jo smiled. She was the cat with the cream, the girl who'd got her man. 'Yes,' she said.

'Be careful,' Susie warned. 'Just imagine if you got pregnant.'

Jo shrugged. 'I won't get pregnant. Are you going to tell the others?'

'I don't have to,' Susie said. 'It's obvious.'

Susie would tell everyone.

During the morning, Jo kept her head down, aware of whispered conversations and looks in her direction. The others could say what they liked about her and Ian. She was proud to be his girlfriend.

At lunchtime, she caught the lift downstairs and went out into Collins Street. Fallen leaves from the plane trees lay on the pavement. She walked through them, hurrying past the Windsor Hotel and around the corner into Spring Street, where Ian stood waiting. He grabbed her hand, and they crossed over the road to the Treasury gardens.

In the gardens they found a vacant seat under the bare branches of a large tree and sat down. Jo opened her handbag and took out her cheese and pickle sandwich. Traffic roared along Spring Street, and high above, clouds floated across the sky.

'Everyone knows about us,' Jo said. 'Susie asked me. I reckon the rest of the office knew in about half an hour.'

Ian put a hand on her leg. 'Can you cope with the gossip?'

She nodded.

'Are you sure?'

'I'm fine.' Her earlier defiance had turned into a feeling of being exposed.

'Maureen guessed as well. She's my big sister.'

Ian unwrapped his sandwich. 'What did you tell her?'

'That you're really good-looking and twenty-eight.'

Ian raised his eyebrows. 'Are you bothered that I'm older?'

'No,' she said. 'But my family will be surprised.'

He smiled. 'Appalled, you mean. They'll think I'm a seducer.'

Jo pushed a fallen leaf aside with her foot. 'My family's old-fashioned. They're Catholic.'

'I understand,' Ian said. He bit into his sandwich.

Surprised, she asked, 'Are you Catholic?'

Ian shook his head. 'I haven't been to mass since I was fourteen. What about you?'

'I haven't been for a year.'

When Jo's mum found out, she said, 'You've abandoned the church so don't expect God to look after you.'

God hadn't looked after Mum, even though she prayed the rosary and went to mass on Sundays and holy days. She'd had five pregnancies and lost two babies at birth. In the hospital she'd been told to forget them, to go home and try again. Sometimes she said, 'If I knew where they were I'd take flowers and have a plaque made. Patrick and Frances. In loving memory. I wasn't allowed to hold them before they were taken away, not even given a snip of their hair. It was a cruel thing to do to a young woman.'

'Do you believe in abortion?' Ian asked.

Startled, Jo said, 'I haven't thought about it.'

'But you were taught that abortion is a mortal sin.'

Jo looked down at the uneaten sandwich in her hand. 'I worked with a girl who had one. She said her grandma came to her in a dream and told her the baby was with her in heaven.'

'It was a guilt dream,' Ian said. He picked up Jo's cold hand and squeezed it. 'Don't worry, I'm careful. You won't have to face that.'

What would happen if one of his condoms broke?

'Sorry, I didn't mean to get serious,' Ian said. 'How about we go out Wednesday night? I'll take you to my favourite Italian restaurant.'

She wondered if he'd taken Ange there. 'I really liked that souvlaki,' she said. 'Can we go to a Greek one?'

He grinned. 'Of course. I like variety in my life.'

She shot him a look. 'As long as it's not women.'

He touched her face. 'I only want you.'

'And I only want you,' she said quietly.

He smiled. 'Good.'

When they finished eating, she said, 'Who's going back first?'

'You are, if you're quick.'

She jumped up from the bench, hurrying towards Spring Street.

'Hey, not so fast.'

He caught up with her and grabbed her hand. They kissed, and she didn't care who saw them, not even Mr Cleary.

...

Ian watched Jo as she walked away. He liked the unselfconscious way she moved. Several men were looking at her. He felt extraordinarily lucky that she wanted him. As he crossed Spring Street, he wondered how things would play out at work. So far, the men didn't know, but they would soon. Moira would be sure to tell them. She reminded Ian of his mum. She had the look of someone who'd endured a lot, patiently.

...

The next morning Jo arrived early at work. As she hung up her jacket, Moira appeared in the doorway of the girls' room.

'Jo, can we talk?'

Jo's heart thumped as she followed Moira across the empty office. If Moira had a go at her about Ian, she'd tell her to mind her own business.

Moira's work area was around the corner from Mr O'Shaughnessy's cubicle. A filing cabinet stood next to the window. On top of the filing cabinet was a mug, with World's Best Mum printed in blue on the side. Moira's son Kenny was seventeen, extremely quiet, and an apprentice baker.

Moira looked up at Jo, her face filled with concern. 'There's gossip going round that you and Ian are going out. Is it true?'

Jo smiled. 'Yes.'

'Please be careful. He's ten years older than you and divorced. He's had a lot of life experience that you haven't.'

'He's nice,' Jo said.

Moira nodded. 'Yes, he is, but he's a man and you're a teenage girl.'

'But—'

'All I'm saying is, people know,' Moira said quietly. 'I've told them not to gossip but don't be surprised if you get remarks. Some of those girls are quite capable of saying unpleasant things. Feel free to come and talk to me if they upset you. I'll try and stop it.'

Jo wouldn't complain whatever the other girls said. She wouldn't give them the satisfaction.

Moira put a hand on Jo's arm. 'You'll bear the brunt of the gossip, but it'll be a nine-day wonder. Just wait and see.'

'Thanks,' Jo said. She went to her desk, sat down and lit a cigarette. Her skin prickled.

The office door opened and closed, and Ian walked in. He looked across at her and smiled. She smiled back. He was her lover, the most important person in the world. She glanced around, caught Nola watching her.

After morning teatime, Jo went into the kitchen. Nola stood at the sink, filling a glass with water. From the office came the sound of typewriters clacking and Judith's loud voice on the switchboard.

Nola turned off the tap. 'Why on earth is a young girl like you going out with a divorced man?' she said. 'Find a nice boy your own age, not someone who'll use you up and throw you away.'

It was none of Nola's business, but Jo forced herself to say politely, 'You don't have to worry. I'm fine.' She walked out of the kitchen. As she went past Ruth's desk Ruth looked up and smiled. Moira and Nola thought they were helping, but Ruth was her friend.

...

Jo lay in bed brooding. A weekend without Ian stretched ahead. She should have arranged to do something with Ruth. Maybe she still could. She slid out of bed and padded to the phone. Ruth's number rang out. *Damn.*

Jo went back to the bedroom and pulled on her jeans and a white jumper. Voices came along the hall. Another of Kathleen's arguments with Mum.

'You're stuck in a time warp,' Kathleen said. 'It's my life and I'm going to do what I want.'

'Don't expect me to pay for you,' Monica said. 'I left school at fourteen and it hasn't done me any harm.'

'It has but you don't recognise it,' Kathleen snapped. 'You're so narrow-minded.'

'People who think they're more important than others are heading for a fall,' Monica said in her doomsday voice.

'I don't think I'm more important than anyone else,' Kathleen said. 'I'm a socialist.'

'Don't use those clever words on me, miss!'

Jo went into the kitchen. Monica sat at the table spreading orange marmalade on her toast, covering it to the edges. Watching her set Jo's teeth on edge.

'Socialist isn't a clever word,' Kathleen said. 'It's an ideology that—'

'Girls don't need an education,' Monica said. 'They get married and have children. If you must get educated, why can't you be a teacher or a nurse?'

Kathleen made a snorting noise. 'Wiping snotty noses and shitty bums? No thanks. I'm going to study science.'

'Science isn't a girl's subject,' Monica said. 'And don't swear.'

Kathleen scowled. 'A scientist can be a man *or* a woman. All you need is the education.'

Jo went to the cupboard and got out a bowl and the Corn Flakes packet. Everything was the wrong way round in this place. Mum should be proud of Kathleen, but the only person she seemed proud of was Maureen.

Monica turned to Jo as if she'd just noticed her. 'What are *you* doing this weekend? Going out with mystery man, I suppose. When are we going to meet him?'

The lie slipped off Jo's tongue easy as anything. 'He's gone camping this weekend.'

'In this weather? What's wrong with him?'

'Nothing,' Jo said. She tipped Corn Flakes into a bowl.

Monica stared at her. 'Is there something you're not telling me?'

'No,' Jo said. She sat down and poured milk over her cornflakes.

'You might get a decent boyfriend if you stopped wearing those awful jeans.'

'I wear what I like.' Jo began spooning cornflakes into her mouth.

'She looks good,' Kathleen added.

Monica glared at Jo. 'Since you're home this weekend, you can take Rufus for a walk and tidy your bedroom.'

Jo frowned. 'It's Maureen's clothes on the floor, not mine.'

'Maureen's gone to work. It won't do you any harm to tidy up. And get that sulky look off your face.'

Jo finished her Corn Flakes and took her bowl to the sink. The weekend was going downhill fast, and she wouldn't see Ian until Monday. How was she going to stand it?

Kathleen pushed back her chair. 'I'm off to the pool.'

'You'll catch your death,' Monica said.

'No, I won't,' Kathleen said, and left, banging the door behind her.

Jo shrugged on her coat and clipped Rufus's lead onto his collar. Outside, the wind tossed her hair and turned Rufus's ears inside out. They went up the street past the silent houses, Rufus pulling on the lead. Jo pulled back, forcing him to slow down. Having a fling was harder than she'd expected. She hated being left alone every second weekend. Apart from having to lie to her mother, it was hard to ignore the feeling that she was nothing more to him than a warm body in his bed. Soon, he'd tell her it was over.

She went around the block with Rufus and returned to the house. In her bedroom, she stared at her miserable reflection in the mirror then put *Look at Us* onto her turntable. Turning up the volume, she went over to the dressing table. Maureen's bottles of perfume stood at the back. Jo chose *Intimate* and squirted it onto her wrists before picking up Maureen's clothes from the floor. Too bad if some of them were clean. They were all going into the wash.

Chapter Nine

That same Saturday morning, Ian drove to Werribee to pick up Anna. As soon as she was in the car she said, 'Guess what, Daddy? Mummy and Martin are going to take me to Tassie for Christmas, and we're going on the ferry.'

Ian felt a surge of anger. This year it was his turn to get Anna for Christmas. He glanced at her excited face and decided to keep quiet. December was months away, but the fact that Ange was making plans for Anna at Christmas when she knew it was his turn grated.

'Are we seeing Elaine?' Anna asked.

Ian started the car and put on the indicator. 'Sweetie, I don't see Elaine anymore.'

Anna's eyes opened wider. 'Did you have a fight?'

He felt guilty. She'd seen enough fighting in her short life. 'No,' he said.

'Did you cheat on her?'

Ian's jaw tightened as he drove up the street. Where did she get that from? Ange, of course. Cheating wasn't a child's word. But he needed to stay calm. 'No.'

'Did she cheat on you?'

'No,' he said. 'We just wanted different things.'

Anna frowned. 'I don't understand.'

'You won't until you're older,' he said, remembering how annoying those words could be to a child, for he'd heard them himself. But he had no other way of explaining. She sat with her knees together and a resigned look on her face. Sometimes he thought she was an old soul.

As Ian drove towards his mum's place at Alphington, an image of Jo's naked body came into his mind. She was so beautiful. An uneasy feeling lurked in his gut. What if she went out tonight and found someone else? How was this going to work? In his pocket was a piece of paper with Jo's phone number on it. He'd give her a call tomorrow.

...

The phone rang late on Sunday afternoon. Jo ran out into the hall and picked it up.

'Jo?'

She gripped the phone tighter. 'Yes.'

'I miss you,' Ian said.

Her heart lifted. 'I miss you too.' She slid down the wall until she sat on the carpet, knees up to her chest.

'What have you been doing?' he asked.

'Not much. I took Rufus for a walk.' She wouldn't add that she'd watched *Go!* as she lay on the couch, smoking and eating potato chips, and tried on some of Maureen's clothes while she was at work, although they didn't look as good on her as they did on Maureen.

Jo had also sorted her clothes into the ones she'd keep and the ones she'd throw out. Mum said she spent far too much money on them and why wasn't she putting together a glory box, like Maureen? Jo had no intention of having a glory box. It would always be second best to Maureen's.

Jo's old school reports were in a shoe box at the top of the wardrobe, including one that said she was smart enough to get a bursary to become a teacher, and should stay at school, and the one from Year 9 that said she tended to question authority and needed to learn acceptance. During Year 9 she discovered boys and cigarettes, hiking up her skirts and undoing the top buttons on her blouses after she'd left the house. But she was still the classic good girl until she fell in love with Robert.

'I wouldn't mind being there right now,' Ian said.

She giggled. 'No, you wouldn't. My family's here. Has Anna gone home?'

'Yes,' Ian said. 'I can come and pick you up if you're not doing anything. We could go to the drive-in.'

'That would be nice.'

'You sound unsure. Are you scared of me meeting your family?'

She thought he sounded amused. 'I'm terrified.'

'Even if they hate me, they can't lock you up,' he said. 'You're old enough to make up your mind.'

'I have,' Jo said.

'Good. See you soon.'

'See you soon.' Jo held the phone to her chest as an unwelcome thought flashed through her mind. Had he rung to find out if she was home? Of course not, she was being paranoid, he'd wanted to ask her out. Anyway, he'd said she was free to go out with anyone she wanted.

At seven o'clock, a knock sounded on the front door. Jo jumped up from her armchair and rushed into the hall. She felt sick with dread. What if Mum asked him about camping? Why had she told that stupid lie? Jo switched on the porch light and opened the door. Ian stood there smiling. He wore a jacket and pants and a dark red polo neck. 'Come in,' she said softly.

Ian stepped inside and they kissed.

In the living room, a fire burned in the wood heater and a Kevin Dennis ad played on the TV. Monica sat on the gold-coloured couch with her knitting while Kev lounged in a chair with his cardigan unbuttoned, a cigarette in one hand.

'Mum and Dad, this is Ian,' Jo said in her most polite voice. If her parents embarrassed her, she'd never forgive them.

Monica stared at Ian so suspiciously that Jo felt a wild urge to shout, 'Yes! We're screwing our arses off!'

Ian walked over to Kev, and they shook hands.

'Kev,' he said. He nodded towards Jo's mum. 'Monica.'

'Nice to meet you,' Ian said.

'Hello,' Monica said. Her voice sounded cold.

Jo cringed inside.

Maureen came in wearing stretchy black pants and a black jumper. She smiled at Ian, putting on her salon charm. 'Hello, I'm Maureen.'

Jo held her breath. Would she ask him about his camping trip?

Ian smiled. 'Ian. Hello.'

Did he sound impressed? She had to get him out of here. 'We'd better go,' she said.

'Where are you going?' Maureen asked.

'The drive-in.'

'What are you going to see?'

'*Dr Zhivago.*'

'Ooh, Omar Sharif. He's such a star.'

Was Maureen spinning this out deliberately, or was she trying to ease the atmosphere?

'We have to go,' Ian said.

'Nice to meet you,' Kev said to Ian. 'See you again.'

Jo felt a tiny glow of warmth. Dad had always been on her side from the time she'd been a little girl, his shed a haven where she ate chocolate biscuits and played with a pair of plastic elephants. When she got older and Mum's nagging got worse, Dad took her aside and said that Mum was too harsh with her, and she should try not to get upset by it. Jo felt as if he'd thrown her a lifeline.

Ian grabbed Jo's hand as they went down the path. Jo fanned her hot face. 'I'm glad that's over.'

'Your dad was friendly,' Ian said. 'But I don't think I won over your mother.'

'She's prejudiced. Only a good Catholic boy will do for me.'

'And I'm an atheist.' Ian opened the passenger door of his car.

Jo got in. She watched Ian as he walked around to the other side of the car.

He opened the door, slid into his seat and started the engine.

'You told me you were lapsed,' she said.

'Lapsed into atheism,' Ian said. 'Is that a problem?'

'No.' It wasn't quite true.

'What about you? Do you believe in God?'

'I don't know.'

Ian glanced at her as he drove up the street. 'That's a nice, safe answer.'

'Why did you stop believing in God?' Jo asked.

'I decided to believe in what I saw around me, not something unseen.'

'I sometimes wonder if God exists,' Jo said.

'You don't have to say it to please me,' Ian said. 'I like you as you are.'

'You don't know much about me.'

He gave her a quick glance. 'I know you're eighteen and beautiful and you've got an operation scar on your right side.'

She started. 'How did you know?'

'Easy. Moira told me you had a kidney operation. And you protect your right side and try very hard to keep it hidden from me.'

Jo's face warmed. 'There are two scars.'

Ian pulled into the kerb under a streetlight and turned off the engine. 'Let me see.'

Jo unbuttoned her jacket with clumsy fingers and lifted her jumper. She unzipped her jeans, pulled them open and turned away from him, then almost gasped when she felt his fingers on her scars. He bent down and kissed them. 'I want all of you,' he said. 'Including the scars.'

She blinked away tears as she zipped up her jeans and pulled down her jumper.

He started the car and drove up the street.

'How many kids in your family? he asked.

'Three girls,' she said. 'Maureen's the oldest, I'm in the middle and Kathleen's the youngest. How many kids in yours?'

'Two,' he said. 'My sister's ten years older.'

'Are we really going to see *Dr Zhivago*?' Jo asked.

Ian grinned. 'Not really. We'll be on the back seat.'

...

After the movie, Ian drove Jo back to her house and walked her to the front door. The place was in darkness, although he could imagine Jo's dragon mother lying awake, listening for the sound of her key in the lock.

'See you tomorrow,' he said quietly.

'Tomorrow,' she echoed.

They kissed.

Driving home, Ian reflected on the fact that Jo was more sensitive than she appeared. He felt a momentary unease. *How was this going to end?*

...

The alarm sounded at six-thirty. Jo groaned and opened her eyes, leaned over and turned the alarm off. The bedroom was dark. Last night, Ian had reached for her as soon as the movie started. 'I've missed you this weekend,' he'd said. It was on the tip of her tongue to mention that she was willing to come to his flat whenever he liked, and that he'd been the one who hadn't invited her, but she'd kept quiet.

She got out of bed. The room felt icy. She pulled on her dressing gown and opened the door. Light spilled along the hall. Jo went into the kitchen, which smelt of cooked toast. Her mum stood at the sink peeling potatoes and dropping them into a bowl of water. She wore a hairnet over her permed hair, which gave her head a strange, flattened shape. Lines edged her mouth and eyes. Even Nola on a bad day looked better.

Monica stared at Jo. 'What's a man like him doing with a young girl like you? How old is he?'

Jo sat down and reached for a piece of toast. 'Twenty-eight.'

'Have you found out if he's Catholic?'

'No.'

'Haven't you asked?'

Jo lit a cigarette. 'It's not something that's come up.' She felt a desperate urge to laugh and sucked in smoke. Immediately she started coughing.

'You should give those cigarettes away,' Monica said. 'You'll end up like your father. Why can't you be sensible and find a decent boy your own age? I could see straight away he's a playboy. It'll end in tears. And while you're going out with him, you're missing the chance of meeting someone suitable.'

Jo tossed her hair over her shoulder. 'I don't want to meet someone suitable.'

'Just as I thought,' Monica said. 'You're besotted.'

Maureen appeared in the doorway. She wore black salon clothes, her long nails curves of deep pink. She sat down and picked up a slice of toast. 'Why wouldn't Ian want to marry Jo?'

Monica plonked the bowl of potatoes to one side and began cutting up heads of broccoli. 'If he's not married at the age of twenty-eight, he's not the marrying kind.'

Maureen spread honey on her toast. 'There's plenty of men who marry late. Just give him a chance. He seems nice to me.'

Jo gave her a grateful glance.

Monica sniffed. 'I'll believe it when I see it.'

Chapter Ten

Winter sunlight slanted through the open venetians of Ian's bedroom. Jo yawned and stretched. It was Saturday, the start of a perfect weekend, and no-one at home knew she was here. She glanced over at Ian, who lay on his back, dozing. Rolling over she tickled his face with a lock of her hair. His eyes flew open. 'Good morning,' she said. 'How about I cook breakfast?'

He shook his head. 'No, I'll do it.'

'But I want to.'

'You don't have to get all domestic on me.'

She felt as if he'd slapped her.

His fingers brushed her bare arm. 'What would you like?'

'Bacon and eggs.'

'There aren't any.'

She pouted. 'But I *want* them.'

He looked at her and sat up. 'Alright, I'll get some. You stay here. Take a shower if you want.'

He kissed her, pulled on some clothes, and left.

She lay in bed staring at the wall. What did he mean, he didn't want her to get all domestic on him? Did he expect her to hang around the flat like a spare part while he made the bed and took out the garbage? Swinging her legs off the bed she padded into the bathroom.

A pair of pineapple-weave towels with green borders hung over the rack. Opening the bathroom cupboard she spotted two toothbrushes, one child-sized, poking out of a Vegemite jar and next to it Ian's shaving gear and Anna's small hairbrush. A few strands of brown hair were trapped in the bristles. There was nothing of Jo's here, nothing to show that she was part of Ian's life. She went back to the bedroom and fished a pink comb out of her handbag, took it into the bathroom and put it beside Anna's hairbrush.

After showering she went into the living room. The couch looked as if it had come off someone's nature strip. If this was her place, she wouldn't have let it through the door. She walked over to Ian's bookcase and scanned the titles. Pulling out *The Big Sleep*, she read the first page then put it back. Her eyes skimmed over the rest: Asimov's *Foundation* trilogy, *The Man in the High Castle*, *Dune*, a large collection of detective stories, including *A Study in Scarlet*, and *The Hound of the Baskervilles*. He read sci-fi and crime. Once she'd wished for a boyfriend who'd read poetry to her.

In the kitchen, she opened the food cupboard. Among the Weet-bix, sugar and flour were flat packets of spaghetti like the Italians ate, tins of tomatoes and anchovies. A bottle of yellow-green olive oil stood next to a dark brown bottle of vinegar. She opened the fridge and spotted Romano, mozzarella and ricotta cheeses. In the vegetable compartment were green and yellow vegetables she couldn't name. She felt a pang of regret. If she hadn't asked for bacon and eggs, he probably would have cooked something exciting. Why hadn't she kept her mouth shut?

She closed the cupboard door and headed towards Anna's bedroom. A flowered bedspread covered Anna's bed and a puppy pyjama case lay on the pillow. Above the bed was an unframed picture of fairies dancing around red-and-white spotted toadstools. Jo went over to the wardrobe and opened the door. A pale blue party dress with puffed sleeves and a gathered skirt hung on the rack. Anna would look gorgeous in it. Jo slid the door shut and went over to the window, which showed a view of the flats next door. Shells and pieces of sea glass lined the window ledge. Jo picked up a piece of sea glass, smooth and cool in her hand. She imagined rock pooling at Ricketts Point with Ian and Anna looking for limpets and barnacles, scuttling crabs and sea anemones with tentacles fanned out in the clear water. It wasn't going to happen. She felt a prickle of resentment. Putting the sea glass down she went back to the living room.

A key turned in the lock and Ian walked in carrying a brown paper bag. She followed him into the kitchen where he dumped the bag on the table and pulled out a packet of eggs and a flat parcel wrapped in butchers' paper.

'Do you always cook for your girlfriends?' she asked as he unwrapped the bacon.

Ian shook his head. 'No, but I wanted to cook for you.'

Surprised, she asked, 'Why?'

'I felt like it.' Ian bent down and got a frying pan out of the cupboard, plonking it on the stove.

She watched him light the gas. 'I put my comb in the bathroom cabinet, or is that getting too domestic for you?' she said.

Ian shrugged. 'You can leave your stuff anywhere you like.'

'So, I'm your proper girlfriend.'

He added rashers to the pan. 'Of course, you are.'

'It doesn't feel like it. I don't see you when you have Anna, and I haven't met any of your friends. It's like you're keeping me a secret.'

Ian cracked eggs on the side of the pan. 'I'm sorry, I wanted to keep you to myself for a while.'

'Is it because we're having a fling?'

He looked at her. 'Isn't that what you want?'

'I don't know,' she said in a low voice.

His face changed. 'Look, if this isn't working—'

She felt the beginning of panic. 'No, it's fine, I just don't know what to tell Mum and Dad when you have Anna for the weekend.'

The fat on the rashers of bacon had begun to curl at the edge, crisp and brown.

'Maybe you should tell them the truth.'

Jo stared at him in dismay. 'You must be joking. Mum would hit the roof.'

'You worry too much about your mother.'

Jo shrugged. Maybe she did, but how could she stop?

They ate the bacon and eggs sitting at the kitchen table. The bacon was perfectly cooked, the eggs with just the right amount of runniness. Afterwards, Ian opened a packet of biscotti and held it out to her. 'Try one,' he said.

It was delicious.

He reached across to wipe crumbs off her lip with his thumb. 'Italian food is so good,' he said. 'I'd love to take you to Italy one day.'

Her heart soared.

...

In the late afternoon, Ian stood on the platform watching the red train snake out of the station. Jo had insisted on catching it home rather than accepting his offer of a lift. He suspected she'd probably spun some yarn to her family about staying with a girlfriend. She seemed so open, yet she probably told lies. But who was he to disapprove? Climbing the stairs, he walked into the main part of the station. A wintry chill filled the space, and only a couple of places were open, selling tomato soup, hot meat pies and tea in paper cups. Emerging from the station he crossed the road to the tram stop.

This weekend had confirmed his opinion that Jo was smart. She'd told him she was surprised that *Brave New World* and *1984* weren't in his bookcase. He'd said he'd read them both. She'd mentioned she borrowed books from the Athenaeum library and liked reading in bed. He told her beds were for sleeping and fucking, and that you read books in your living room. She'd frowned. 'Not on your couch. It looks like it came off someone's nature strip.'

He'd told her it did, and laughed when she pulled a face.

When they walked on the beach on Sunday she'd hunted for shells, and pieces of sea glass. He'd almost said, 'You and Anna would get on like a house on fire,' before reason kicked in and reminded him that Ange made trouble whenever she knew one of his girlfriends had spent time with Anna. There'd be an auntie coming from interstate or Anna had a birthday party to go to, so she couldn't come on access that weekend. He remembered how frustrated and angry he'd been. If he could, he'd keep Jo away from Anna.

...

The following Sunday, Jo and Ruth walked into an afternoon disco in Little Bourke Street. Coloured lights glowed against the brick walls of the warehouse, a band played out the front and the concrete dance floor heaved with people. Walking up Little Bourke Street, Ruth had said, 'Fingers crossed I'll meet someone without clammy hands or bad breath.'

They giggled, although Jo wasn't in a laughing mood. All week she'd been hoping that Ian would ask her to the flat for the weekend, but he'd said nothing on Friday other than, 'I'll call you on Sunday night, sweetheart.'

When she complained about it to Ruth, she'd said, 'It's not fair you have to stay home just because he's got Anna. Come to the disco with me on Sunday.'

They left their coats and bags in the cloakroom and stepped onto the floor. Almost immediately, a blonde boy walked up to Ruth and held out his hand. He reminded Jo of a boy she'd once liked at school, tall and narrow in the hips. She found an empty seat at the edge of the floor and lit a cigarette, watching Ruth and the blonde boy dancing. He looked like a stick insect, all arms and legs. She wondered what Ian and Anna were doing, and a wave of longing swept through her.

A stocky boy with a groovy haircut came up to Jo and asked for a dance. She stubbed out her cigarette and followed him onto the floor. She began to dance with the boy, and the music took hold of her, like it always did.

He yelled into her ear, 'The band's fab, isn't it?'

Through a gap in the crowd, she saw that the lead singer had taken off his jacket and rolled up the sleeves of his shirt. The shirt was unbuttoned halfway way down his front. Light bounced off the gold medallion on his chest. His voice sounded gravelly, as if he'd smoked too many cigarettes.

She nodded and smiled.

When the band walked off for a break, the boy said, 'I'm Paul.'

'Jo,' she said. 'Excuse me, I'll be back in a minute.'

She joined the queue waiting outside the toilets. When it was her turn, she wrinkled her nose. The toilet was disgusting. Afterwards, she rinsed her hands under the tap. There was no soap, and the loop of cloth for drying hands was sodden, but in the mirror her eyes shone. It surprised her to realise that she was enjoying herself. When she walked into the dance area, Paul waited, two bottles of Coke in his hands.

'Have a Coke,' he said, handing her a bottle.

She took it. 'Thanks.'

Ruth and the blonde boy stood near the edge of the floor. Ruth waved.

'Are they your friends?' Paul asked.

'Ruth is,' Jo said. 'Come and meet her.' She'd drink the Coke, smoke a cigarette and talk about her favourite bands, behave like the girl she'd been before she met Ian. That girl seemed light years away from who she was now.

Three hours later, the four of them walked down to Flinders Street Station. The city cold and grey, shops closed, shadows lengthening as the short afternoon turned to dusk.

They walked behind Ruth and the blonde boy, whose name was Carl. Earlier, Paul had tried to take Jo's hand, but she'd said, 'I'm sorry, I should have told you. I've got a boyfriend.'

Paul had looked around in mock surprise. 'Where is he?'

'He was busy this weekend.'

'What's so important he can't see you?'

She'd never thought of it like that. 'Nothing,' she said.

Paul flicked his fringe off his face, a single movement. 'Does he do this to you a lot?'

She'd tell him because after today she'd never see him again. 'Every second weekend.'

'You should have it out with him. If he's got someone else, give me a call.'

Jo sighed. 'It's not that easy.'

'What's so hard about it?'

'He's seeing his daughter.'

Paul's jaw dropped. 'Are you going out with a married man?'

Jo shook her head. 'Divorced.'

'How old are you?'

'Eighteen.'

'And how old is he?'

'Twenty-eight.'

Paul whistled.

'I s'pose you think I'm stupid,' Jo said.

'I don't know what to think.'

Paul kept glancing at her as they crossed at the lights and walked along Swanston Street. She felt guilty she was wasting his time.

When they arrived, Ruth and Carl went off to catch the train to Footscray, while Paul waited with Jo on the platform. As the train snaked into the station, he fished a pen and a small piece of paper out of his jacket pocket and wrote some numbers down. 'This is my phone number,' he said, handing it to her. 'Give me a call when you and your boyfriend split up.'

'Thanks for a nice afternoon,' she said. 'See you.'

'I hope so,' he said. 'You're beautiful.'

...

At home, Jo was hanging up her coat when Maureen came in. 'Ian rang. I thought you said you were going out with him. Where have you been?'

Jo almost stopped breathing. 'What did you say?'

'I said you were out, and to ring back later,' Maureen said. 'But I want to know where you've been.'

Pots rattled in the kitchen. Jo closed the bedroom door. Mum had ears like a bat. 'I went to a disco in the city with Ruth.'

'Have you and Ian had a fight?' Maureen asked.

'No.'

'I don't understand.'

It felt like a relief to tell Maureen. 'He sees his daughter every second weekend.'

Maureen's expression turned to shock. 'Don't tell me he's married.'

'Divorced. And if you tell Mum I'll hate you forever.'

'Don't be stupid, you know I won't,' Maureen said. 'Why doesn't he let you see her?'

'Because we're only casual. I said it was what I wanted.'

'Is it?'

'No.'

Maureen shook her head. 'You've done it again, haven't you? Picked someone who'll hurt you. How come he's divorced?'

'He doesn't talk about it.'

'If it was me,' Maureen said, 'I'd want to know everything.'

'Well, I don't.'

'Because you might find out something about him you don't like.' Maureen went over to the mirror, examining her face in the glass. 'You really know how to choose them. Fancy expecting you to stay home all weekend.'

'He doesn't,' Jo said. 'I can go out with anyone I want.'

Maureen lifted an eyebrow. 'Well, why don't you?'

The phone rang in the hall. Jo raced out of the bedroom and picked it up.

'Hello.'

'Hello, sweetheart,' Ian said. 'Have you had a good day?'

She twirled the cord of the phone around her finger. 'Yes, I did.'

'What did you do?' His voice sounded light, casual.

'I went out with Ruth.'

'Did you do any fun things?'

'We went to a disco in the city.' Was it her imagination that his voice changed?

'Did you have a good time?'

'Yes.' In the silence she was aware of her heartbeat. *Stuff him.* 'I met someone who wanted to go out with me.'

'What did you say?'

'No.'

Silence, then, 'How about we go away next weekend?' he said.

Surprised, she asked, 'Where?'

'I've got a mate with a house at Skeins Creek. It's along the Great Ocean Road. It'll be empty this time of year.'

A whole weekend in a house, just by themselves. It thrilled her. 'I'd love to,' she said.

She felt him smiling at the other end of the line. 'Marvellous. See you tomorrow.'

'See you tomorrow,' she echoed. She put down the phone, softly.

...

Ian hung up and stepped out of the phone box. He felt as if he'd been punched in the guts. He'd left Jo alone for the weekend, and a boy had asked her out. Luckily she'd said no, but he couldn't let it happen again. If it led to trouble with Ange he'd have to manage.

As Ian walked along the pavement he tried to focus on the weekend at Skeins Creek. The idea had come into his head out of nowhere. The weather would be cold and grey, but he'd take Jo for walks along the beach. Maybe they'd build a fire and toast marshmallows on it. They'd have a romantic weekend. He'd talk to her, promise he'd do his best to make her happy, but there'd be no mention of marriage. It was a trap.

Chapter Eleven

They arrived at the house in Skeins Creek well after dark. Inside, it felt icy, and the air smelt musty, as if the windows and doors hadn't been opened for a long time. Ian switched on the lights and they went into the living room, which was furnished with old red armchairs and a dining setting of dark wood. A low bookcase against a wall held battered paperbacks, jigsaw puzzles and games of Scrabble and Monopoly.

They found tea and coffee on the kitchen bench and a packet of sugar in the larder, along with tins of food and a jar of apricot jam, half used. Their bedroom had a built-in wardrobe with a mirror in the middle.

'That'll be nice,' Ian said. 'We'll be able to watch ourselves.'

Jo cringed inside. Her scars were taking ages to fade, her breasts were too small and her hip bones stuck out. How could Ian think she was beautiful? But to have the entire weekend with him at Skeins Creek was so unexpected, she'd do whatever he wanted.

On the way down she'd felt with each passing mile that they were escaping, she from her family and he from his broken past. When they stopped at a service station, he bought hot dogs and watery coffee in paper cups; they ate and drank in the car as the windows steamed up and rain trickled down the glass.

After they unpacked their bags, they made up the bed with Ian's sheets and blankets, then he took her hand and led her to the mirror. When he began taking off her clothes, she avoided looking at herself.

'What's wrong?' he asked.

'I'm cold,' she said, and it was true, the heater he'd switched on had done little to warm the room.

'Race you to bed,' he said.

She got there first but he grabbed her ankle. Laughing, she kicked out, but he had her ankle in a firm grip. 'Got you.' He climbed onto the bed, and they dived under the covers, where he began stroking her breasts. 'You're so beautiful,' he said.

She felt something different about him, as if he was building up to say something. As she took him in her arms an awful thought came into her head. Had he brought her here to split up?

...

In the morning she woke to the boom of the sea. Ian slept quietly on his back. She lay propped on one elbow, gazing at the wide angles of his face, the dark eyelashes on his cheeks. He woke and reached for her.

While he dozed, she slid out of bed, showered in the icy bathroom, put on her jeans, jumper and a pair of woolly socks, and wandered into the kitchen. Pulling up the blind she stared into the backyard. A scrubby lawn, some wind-battered shrubs and a rusty Hills Hoist at the end of a narrow strip of concrete. In summer it probably looked different, with a barbeque and outdoor furniture. Maybe there'd be a badminton net, or a plastic paddling pool for a child. She wondered if Ian had brought Anna here.

She'd told her mother that she was spending the weekend with Ruth, but Maureen had guessed. 'You're having a weekend with Ian, aren't you?' she'd said. 'Good on you. I could do with a break myself.'

Maureen and Michael were having a house built in the estate behind Mum and Dad's place. So many things had to be chosen, and Maureen was picky. Even Michael, who adored her, got irritated sometimes. 'A tap's just a tap. It turns on and off.'

Maureen fancied herself as a decorator and kept a scrapbook of pictures she'd cut out of *Home Beautiful.* She liked couches and chairs with wooden arms, long coffee tables and low sideboards with sliding glass doors where she could show off her Noritake dinner set. Maureen would get what she wanted. She always did.

Ian walked into the kitchen. He wore pants and his dark red polo neck, and was freshly shaved. He came over and kissed her.

'I'm making some coffee,' Jo said. 'Want some?

'Please.' He sat at the table.

The kettle boiled. She made the coffee and handed him a mug.

'Thanks.' He blew on the surface to cool it.

She sat down opposite. Her throat ached. If he had something on his mind, why the hell didn't he say it? 'Do you want to go to the beach?' she asked.

'Anything you like,' he said. 'This weekend's your treat. I've been neglecting you.'

She looked away from him. 'I felt abandoned,' she said. 'That's why I went out with Ruth.'

He reached for her hand. 'I'm sorry, sweetheart. That's no way to go on.'

Her chest filled with a wild grief. *So, you do want to end it.* She got up and rushed into the bedroom. Flinging open the wardrobe door, she dragged her coat off its hanger.

Ian came into the room. 'What are you doing?'

She thrust her arms into the sleeves of her coat. 'Did you think it was a good idea to bring me down here to end it? It'll take hours for me to get home.'

He put a hand on her arm. 'You've got it wrong. I don't want to end it. Please, don't run away. We need to talk.'

Her heart pounded as she hung her coat back in the wardrobe and stood waiting, aware of the unmade bed that smelt of their lovemaking, the mirror in which she'd seen their naked bodies entwined.

'I think it's time you got to know Anna,' he said.

Jo's mouth dropped open. 'But aren't we just casual?'

Ian sighed. 'I thought that was what I wanted but I was wrong. I want the three of us to spend time together.'

In the silence, wind rattled the window frames.

'I know you'll eventually go off and marry someone else,' Ian continued. 'But while we're together, I'll do my best to make you happy. And I know I sound selfish, but I don't want you going out with other men. I want you for myself. What do you say?'

Was he telling her that he loved her? She wasn't sure. 'I've loved you from the very beginning,' she said.

He smiled. 'It's lust.'

'It's love.'

His smile deepened. 'Put your coat back on. We're going for a walk.'

At the beach the sea mirrored the sky, waves crashing against the shore. A couple of men fished off the rocks and a boy threw a stick along the sand for a black labrador. Seagulls hung overhead, their bodies pale against the clouds.

Jo and Ian walked hand in hand along the wet sand at the water's edge, where seaweed, shells and cuttlefish bones had been cast up by the tide. She scanned the debris, and stopped to pick up a shell, turning it around in her fingers. The shell was tiny, a spiral of tan and white. On the inside, delicate pink. 'Isn't it beautiful?' she said. 'Nature's colours are always best.' She stooped to put the shell down on the sand with the others.

'I'd like you to spend weekends at my flat,' Ian said.

She stood up. 'I can't. Mum would kick me out. I had to lie about this weekend.'

Ian frowned. 'Our relationship can't be built on lies.'

He was right. Lying tainted their relationship. Instantly she knew what to do. 'I'll leave home,' she said.

He smiled. 'That would be marvellous.'

She felt too excited to stay still. Bending down, she pulled off her shoes and socks.

'What are you doing?' Ian asked.

'Catch me.'

She took off, tearing along the edge of the waves, the wind whipping back her hair. The damp sand near the water's edge felt firm under her bare feet, which were turning numb with cold. She glanced over her shoulder, saw Ian rapidly gaining. When he came abreast, she slowed down and stopped, her chest heaving.

He stood facing her. 'You see,' he said softly, 'you want to be free.'

...

As Ian and Jo walked back along the beach, he felt an unusual sense of optimism.

'Promise me one thing,' he said.

She looked up at him her face glowing. 'Anything.'

'That you won't lie again to your mother. Honesty's important.'

She was impressed by his integrity. 'I know. Alright, I promise.'

He smiled. 'Good.'

...

On Monday morning, Ruth came into the girls' room with a quick step, eyes shining.

'Well?' Jo asked as Ruth brushed her hair.

'He turned up,' Ruth said.

'And?'

'We're going out on Wednesday night.'

'He's keen, then.'

Ruth squirted perfume behind her ears, which were small and neat. 'We got on so well. He did most of the talking, and I listened.'

They giggled.

'What did he talk about?' Jo said.

'Himself,' Ruth said. 'Don't all boys do that when they want to impress you?'

'Ian doesn't.'

'Ian already knows you're impressed so he doesn't bother. How was the weekend?'

'Fantastic,' Jo said. 'I'm leaving home.'

Ruth's expression changed to shock. 'Are you moving in with him?'

'Come on,' Jo said. 'No-one does that.'

'Except Moira and Ollie.'

It was hard to believe that sensible, middle-aged Moira lived with quiet, gentle-faced Ollie, even harder to believe they shared the same bed. For years, Moira had been married to a man who'd beaten her. Ian said Moira had probably gone through hell, and he knew what that was like. His face had been grim, so she hadn't dared ask.

'If I earned more money, I'd move out too,' Ruth said. 'I hate living at home since Andy left.'

Andy, Ruth's clever brother, three years older, had gone to study interstate.

Ruth's eyes shone. 'I've just had an idea. How about I ask Mum if you can board at my place? You could have Andy's old room. I'll talk to her if you want.'

Jo clapped her hands together. 'What a fantastic idea. You're brilliant.'

'I'll let you know tomorrow,' Ruth said.

'Fingers crossed,' Jo said. She went out into the office and sat at her desk, feeling a slow-burning excitement. Now that she'd made up her mind, she needed to leave home as soon as possible. Mum would nag her to stay, piling on the guilt. How could Jo think of leaving when Maureen's wedding was only a few months away? It was the most important day of Maureen's life. Well, leaving home was the most important day of Jo's life, not Maureen's wedding.

If Ruth's mum said yes, it would be the first time Jo would have a room of her own. It would be neat, but not sterile. She'd pin a print over the bed, or maybe a painting she'd buy from a street artist. There'd be a white sheepskin rug on the floor. She'd take her record player, records and favourite books, including the ones she'd loved as a child. But now she had to stop thinking about it. Ruth's mum might say no.

Chapter Twelve

The next day when Ruth came in she said, 'You can move in this weekend.'

Jo jumped up from her desk and put her arms around her; they did a funny little dance in front of the typists.

'What's going on?' Susie asked.

'Jo's coming to live at my place,' Ruth said.

Nola frowned. 'Young girls leave home much too early these days. In my time they used to stay home until they were married.'

Jo rushed into Ian's cubicle. 'Ruth's mum said yes.'

'Marvellous,' he said. 'When are you moving in?'

'This weekend.'

'I'll help if you like.'

'I thought you were having Anna.'

Ian shook his head. 'The weekend after. Ange is going away that weekend, so we swapped.'

Jo stood still. She hated any mention of Ange.

'Saturday or Sunday?' Ian asked.

'Saturday afternoon,' Jo said. She pulled a face. 'I'll tell my family tonight.'

'It might be hard, sweetheart, but you're only there 'til Saturday. And I'm coming to pick you up.'

He was her knight in shining armour, riding in to rescue her. 'Thank you,' she said.

...

When Jo got home, Maureen had gone out with Michael, and Kathleen was on the phone to one of her weird friends. When she hung up, Jo beckoned her into the bedroom.

'What's up?' Kathleen asked.

'I'm leaving on Saturday.'

'That's a surprise. Where are you going?'

'Footscray. I'm boarding with Ruth.'

'Good for you,' Kathleen said. 'I didn't know you had the guts.'

At teatime, Jo sat at the kitchen table, picking at her food – corned silverside with white sauce, mashed potatoes and peas. Everyone was in a good mood, and she was going to wreck it. 'I'm leaving home,' she said.

Maureen stared, while Monica's fork stopped in mid-air. 'When?'

'Saturday.'

'What on earth for?' Monica said. 'You've got a perfectly good home here.' Her voice hardened. 'It's because of Ian, isn't it?'

'Yes,' Jo said.

Monica flashed a triumphant glance at Kev. "I knew this would happen. I said to your father the other day he'll try and sweet talk you into leaving home.'

Jo glanced at her dad. His face had gone pale.

'Where are you going?' he asked.

'Footscray. I'm boarding with Ruth and her mum.' Jo glared at Monica. 'You don't have to worry, they're both Catholic.'

'You mark my words,' Monica said in an icy voice, 'when he's finished with you, he'll throw you away like a piece of rubbish.'

'He won't. He loves me.'

'So, he's planning to marry you, is he?'

'I don't know.'

Monica folded her arms. 'I thought not.'

'Give him a break,' Kathleen said. 'They've only been going out for a few months.'

Monica glared at Jo. 'I knew the moment I met him he was a playboy.'

Jo pushed back her chair and stood up. 'He's *not* a playboy. Why can't you just be *fair* to him for once?' She stormed along the hall to her bedroom, slamming the door.

A minute or so later, Kathleen's voice said, 'Can I come in?'

Jo got up from her bed and opened the door.

Kathleen slipped inside. 'Take no notice of Mum,' she said. 'She's jealous because you're doing things she wouldn't dare do herself.'

It was a heady thought.

'When she starts talking to you again, she'll try and change your mind,' Kathleen said. 'Don't listen.'

'As if,' Jo said.

'They hugged, drew apart, smiled at each other.

...

Monica stood with her arms crossed watching Jo pack her clothes. Rufus lay on the carpet nearby, sad-eyed, his nose on his paws. Jo could scarcely bring herself to look at him. He'd always been her special boy, the one who understood how she was feeling. Leaving him would break her heart.

'I've done my best to raise you as a good Catholic girl and this is my reward,' Monica said. 'Don't come running home to me if you get into trouble.'

Jo slammed down the lid on the grey suitcase. *I bloody won't.*

'Don't forget I want that suitcase back,' Monica said. 'What time is he coming?'

'Two.'

'You'll have to be careful in a place like Footscray. It's dangerous.'

Jo shoved her shoes into a large paper bag. 'What makes you think Noble Park's safe? Someone got stabbed at the dance on Friday night.'

'I'm sure there are plenty more stabbings in Footscray.'

Kathleen appeared in the doorway. 'No, just Franco Cozzo.'

They giggled.

Monica frowned. 'It's not funny.'

Jo pulled out her box of records from under the bed.

'I won't miss those,' Kathleen said.

Last night she'd beckoned Jo into her room and closed the door.

'Whatever happens with Ian, promise me you'll stay in Melbourne,' she said. 'This place isn't good for you.'

'I know,' Jo said. 'I promise.'

A knock sounded on the front door. Jo jumped up and hurried down the hall. Rufus trotted after her.

'He can come in and have a cup of tea,' Monica called after her.

Jo opened the door. Ian stood on the porch. He stepped inside and kissed her. 'Are you ready?'

'Yes, but Mum wants us to have a cup of tea.'

Ian lifted an eyebrow. 'Wants?'

'Will you?' Jo asked.

'Alright, just for a few minutes.'

In the kitchen, Rufus sneaked under the table near Jo while Monica spooned tea into the pot. Jo sat down next to Ian, felt the warmth as his knee touched hers under the table.

'Where's Kev?' Ian asked.

'He had to stay back at work.' Monica poured boiling water into the pot and put on the lid.

Jo wanted to scream. Everything was happening slowly: Kathleen getting out the teacups, saucers and plates, and putting them on the table, followed by the milk jug and bowl of sugar, opening the biscuit tin and layering Custard Creams and Monte Carlos onto a plate. The pattern on the plate was an old-fashioned one called Blue Willow. Jo remembered eating scones off it when she came home from primary school.

Monica sat at her end of the table with the teapot. She looked at Ian, her face radiating dislike. 'Do you take milk and sugar?'

'Milk, please, just a tiny bit. No sugar.'

Monica poured his tea and sloshed in a large dollop of milk. The tea slopped over the rim of the cup as she pushed it across the table. 'Well,' she said. 'My daughter's moving out today. I hope you're satisfied.'

Jo's skin prickled. This was excruciating.

Ian's face was expressionless as he looked down at the spilt tea in his saucer. 'It's Jo's choice.' He took a clean hankie out of his pants pocket and mopped it up.

Monica shook her head. 'You've persuaded her.'

'It was my idea,' Jo said.

Kathleen picked up the plate of biscuits. 'Biscuit, anyone?'

Jo shook her head, but Ian took a Custard Cream and bit into it. Under the table Rufus whined. Kathleen fed him a biscuit.

'No good will come of this,' Monica said in her best doomsday voice.

Unexpectedly, her face fell. 'You're my first baby to leave home. I didn't think it would happen so soon.'

Amid her frustration and sadness, Jo felt a stab of guilt. 'I'll come back I swear.'

'I hope so.' Monica glared at Ian. 'My daughter cares for you very much. Make sure you're worthy of her.'

Jo's eyes opened wider. Mum had said something nice about her. An unwanted image slid into her head, of Mum smiling as she put Jo's homemade birthday cake, with seven pink candles, on the kitchen table.

'I do care for Jo,' Ian said. 'Probably more than you think.'

'Another biscuit?' Kathleen said to Ian.

Ian swallowed the last of his tea. 'No thanks. We'd better be going.'

'Not yet,' Monica said. 'I haven't finished. You've no intention of marrying her, have you? You're not the marrying kind.'

'I was eight years ago,' Ian said in a cold voice. 'We got a divorce.'

Monica's mouth dropped open. She stared at Jo. 'Did you know he's divorced?'

'Yes,' Jo said. 'And I don't care.'

Monica's eyes narrowed to slits as she glared at Ian. 'Get out of my house.'

'For heaven's sake, Mum, stop being so melodramatic,' Kathleen said.

Ian stood up. 'Come on, sweetheart, let's go.'

Monica stabbed a finger at Jo. 'If you go with him, you're no daughter of mine.'

A knock sounded on the front door.

'I'll get it,' Monica said.

'Come on,' Ian said. 'Let's get out of here.'

Jo, Ian and Kathleen went into Jo's bedroom.

Voices came down the hall, then Monica and Robbie, the neighbour from over the road, stood in the doorway.

'Jo, is it a good idea to leave like this?' Robbie said. 'Your mother's upset.'

'I'm going to board with my Catholic friend and all Mum can do is shout abuse at Ian,' Jo said.

'You're a sensible girl,' Robbie said. 'Why don't we go into the kitchen, and talk?'

'No,' Jo said. 'I'm going now.'

'Don't listen to *me*,' Monica said. 'Don't believe anything *I* say.'

Kathleen made a face. 'Shut up, Mum. You're making it worse.'

Monica and Robbie retreated to the kitchen while the others carried Jo's things to Ian's car. Rufus wandered in and out of the house, a confused look on his face. Jo felt a wild urge to take him with her.

Ian stowed the last of Jo's things in the boot. 'Right,' he said. 'Let's go.'

Jo put her arms around Kathleen. 'I'll stay in touch, I promise.'

'You'd better,' Kathleen said.

Jo bent down to hug Rufus. Tears ran down her cheeks and dripped onto his fur. 'I'm going to miss you, sweet boy.'

Seconds later, she was in the car with Ian. Pulling her hankie out of her handbag she mopped her face. 'I'm so upset.'

Ian put a hand on her thigh. 'You've every right to be. Your mother was completely over the top. I'm proud of you, sweetheart. Now you can live your life how you want.'

'I wish I could have brought Rufus.'

'He's better off where he is,' Ian said. 'It's no life for a dog being shut in a flat all day.'

Jo looked back just before they turned the corner. Her mum and Robbie stood on the nature strip with Kathleen and Rufus, the four of them getting smaller by the second.

At Ian's flat, he opened the fridge and took out a bottle of Barossa Pearl. She knew he'd bought it especially for her because he preferred red wine. Opening it, he poured the sparkling wine into two glasses, handing one to Jo. He picked up his own. 'Here's to us.'

They clinked glasses.

'To us,' Jo echoed.

'Drink up,' Ian said. 'We're going to St Kilda.'

Her stomach warmed with the alcohol. 'Where in St Kilda?'

'It's a surprise.'

In St Kilda they walked past smoky cafes filled with sad-eyed men drinking coffee, and a pregnant girl with dyed-blonde hair wearing a dress that showed the slope of her breasts and roundness of her belly. Posters on run-down buildings advertised upcoming shows at the Palais, and a couple of drunks slept in a doorway. Everything seemed strange and exciting.

Ian took her to Monarch Cakes in Acland Street, where they ate Polish baked cheesecake, then they walked to the St Kilda foreshore and out along the pier where some men and boys dangled fishing rods into the water. Dark clouds piled overhead, and waves slapped against the pylons. Ian's hand felt warm in hers.

He gazed out over the sea. 'We should go on the ferry to Tassie,' he said. 'Spend a few days there.'

Jo's eyes shone. 'That'd be marvellous.'

It was probably a dream. Ian was always short of money. He'd told her that before he married, he'd wanted to go overseas. She'd wanted to go herself, but after her operation, her savings account was empty. Still, they had each other, just like Sonny and Cher.

...

Jo and Ian arrived at Ruth's place at teatime. The milk bar was open. It looked the same as the milk bar in Noble Park, with Peter's Ice Cream and Four'N Twenty pie signs on the wall. A fluorescent tube hanging from the ceiling lit the space with cold light. Ruth's mum stood behind the counter. She had the same reddish hair and anxious expression as Ruth, but her body had filled out to plumpness. A faded floral apron was tied around her middle.

'Hello, Jo,' she said, then looked at Ian, who had put Jo's grey suitcase on the floor.

'I'm Ian,' he said. 'Jo's boyfriend.'

Ruth's mum stared at him. 'I'm Betty. Pleased to meet you.' When she came out from behind the counter, Jo saw that she wore brown slippers with zips up the front. She went to a shabby curtain at the back of the shop and jerked it open. 'Ruth, Jo's here.'

Ruth appeared, looking hot and flustered.

'Don't just stand there,' Betty said. 'Help Jo with her things.'

They went outside and unpacked the boot, then carried Jo's possessions upstairs to Andy's bedroom. The old wooden bed was covered with a green bedspread that had been turned back, exposing green blankets, white sheets that had been neatly patched and a single knobbly pillow. An old wardrobe with a piece of oval glass in the middle stood along one wall and the curtains had been drawn across the window. The room felt icy.

Ian dumped the suitcase on the rug. 'I'd better go.'

'Why don't you stay and have tea,' Ruth said. 'I'm cooking a roast.'

Ian shook his head. 'That's very nice of you but your mother hasn't asked me.'

They went downstairs to the milk bar.

'I'll be off, then,' Ian said to Betty. 'See you later.'

'Bye,' Betty said, giving him another stare.

Jo went with him out to the car.

'See you tomorrow,' he said, bending his head to kiss her.

She breathed in the warm smell of his hair and skin, the dampness of his wool jacket.

When she came inside, Ruth's mum said, 'I'd like you to treat this place as your home. There are rules, of course. I expect you to keep your room clean, not to smoke in bed, and when you go out at night to come home at a decent hour. Your board includes your food, and you can use the washing machine and clothesline out the back. And I don't want any hanky-panky. Ian can come and visit, but he must stay downstairs.'

Jo's cheeks flamed. 'I understand,' she said.

She went upstairs and fetched her purse; when she handed it over, Betty counted out the money and slipped it into the pocket of her apron. 'Thank you, dear,' she said. 'I'm sure we'll get along fine.'

...

Maureen called Jo at work on Monday. 'You and Ian have ruined everything,' she said. 'Mum says you can't be my bridesmaid. Why did Ian have to tell her he was divorced?'

'Ian's very honest,' Jo said.

'Mum went to see Father Brady last night,' Maureen continued. 'He might talk her into being more reasonable. I mean, Ian's not going to marry you, is he?'

Jo slammed down the phone.

In the middle of the room, Nola startled, and looked at her.

Sorry, Jo mouthed. Lighting a cigarette, she stared through the window. On a nearby rooftop, a pair of sheets hung on a sagging clothesline. Jo inhaled and blew out smoke. Maureen only thought of herself, and Mum had her priorities wrong. She hated Ian but she'd have been thrilled if Jo went out with Barry from Catholic youth club. Barry drank like a fish and screwed girls on the back seat of his car, but he was Catholic, so it was alright.

Her phone rang. She lifted the receiver. 'Hello, Jo speaking.'

'What's going on?' Ian asked. 'You look like you could explode.'

'Maureen called. She said Mum won't let me be a bridesmaid.'

'Lucky you,' Ian said.

Didn't he understand what it meant? 'I feel like an outcast,' Jo said.

'Better than letting your family rule your life.'

How could he be so callous? 'I love my family.'

'I'm sure you do.'

'I can't help it if my mum's a pain.'

'No, you can't, but you're free now.'

She didn't feel it.

...

Ian watched Jo as she went back to her desk. It was a good thing Monica had disowned her. It might give her the chance to break away. Monica was a domineering old bag who thought she was right about everything. One day, and he hoped soon, Jo would be able to see that. Kids could get their parents so wrong.

Ian had been nineteen when he met his father by accident in Swanston Street. His father stood at a fruit stand, buying oranges, but Ian recognised him instantly despite not laying eyes on him for years. Ian had always imagined his father would have become a broken-down alcoholic by now, slumped in a doorway and swigging port from a flagon, but he looked healthy, with clear skin and only a few broken veins on his cheeks. Ian's heart thudded as he said, 'Dad.'

Ian's father took his bag of oranges from the vendor and turned, a startled expression on his face. 'Ian?'

Ian's guts lurched. 'Yes, it's me.'

'It's been a long time,' his father said.

'Twelve years.' This was the moment Ian had been waiting for. He'd often imagined a scene in which his father would say how much he'd missed him and would like for them to make a fresh start.

Ian's father stroked his chin. 'A lot of water's gone under the bridge, son.' His eyes followed a tram rumbling past. 'Sorry, got to go. It's my lunch hour.'

Ian felt a surge of anger. No mention of another meeting, no asking after Ian's sister Tricia. 'I thought the drink would have killed you by now.'

'Got off it after I left your mother,' his father said. 'Proudest day of my life.'

'Why did you leave?' Ian asked as his father started walking off.

'Your bitch of a mother was dragging me down,' his father said over his shoulder.

Ian's anger blazed white hot. Why had he spent so long pining for this selfish, lying prick to come back? He'd treated Ian's mum like a slave, slapped her about when he got drunk.

'You're a fucking liar,' Ian said, ignoring several shocked looks from people walking past. Later, he went to the pub and got drunk, wanting to forget how badly he'd behaved towards his mum after his father left, blaming her for it, until Billy from next door took him in hand, told him only a coward hits a woman, never a man, and he needed to remember that. And Ian did, but it didn't prevent him from betraying Ange, even though she deserved it.

Chapter Thirteen

Jo stood on Ian's balcony smoking. It was a bare windswept space, the wrought iron railings rusting in the salty air. Ian had gone to pick up Anna for the weekend, and Jo knew nothing about kids. Ian had said not to worry, that Anna would think she was fab. Jo wasn't so sure.

Down below, Ian's car swung into the drive. Jo could just see the small shape of Anna sitting next to him in the passenger seat. Her stomach fluttered. It was going to be the longest weekend in her life. She stubbed out her cigarette and went into the living room.

A few minutes later, the front door opened, and Ian and Anna walked in. 'Here's Jo,' he said. 'Anna, you remembered her from the ice-rink, didn't you?'

Anna nodded, her dark eyes on Jo's face. She was as beautiful as Jo remembered.

Jo smiled. 'Hello, Anna.'

Anna looked up at her. 'Hello.'

Jo squirmed inside.

'How about putting your things in your room, and we'll get going,' Ian said.

Anna raced into her bedroom.

'She wants to see her grandma before we go to the zoo,' Ian said quietly. 'So, I said yes. We can't start the weekend with her in a bad mood.'

Jo wore jeans and a tight jumper, and on her feet were black boots with zips up the side. She should have worn a dress, with a longer skirt than usual. 'It's fine,' she said.

Anna raced out, eyes shining. 'Are you ready?'

In the car, Ian talked with Anna while Jo sat silently beside him. Anna told him that she wanted a pink bike for her birthday. 'Mummy and Martin are buying it.'

Jo watched Ian's expression turn stony. She was starting to read his expressions, could see how angry he was. It made her want to reach out and touch him, but she didn't know how he'd react.

...

Ian grabbed Jo's hand as they walked along the path to his mother's house. 'You don't have to worry,' he said. 'It'll be fine.'

Jo said nothing.

The front door opened as they went up the steps. Ian's mum was shorter than Jo by a head. She smiled as Anna ran towards her. 'Hello, love. Give your grandma a kiss.'

When she straightened, Ian said, 'Mum, this is Jo.'

Ian's mum smiled at Jo. 'Hello dear. Call me Mary. Come in.'

The house was dark and old-fashioned, with flowery carpet in the hall and a musty smell. The kitchen was painted pale green and a plate of butterfly cakes sat on a plate in the middle of the table.

'Have a seat,' Mary said.

Jo sat next to Ian on one of the vinyl chairs. Under the table he pushed his knee against hers. She hadn't fooled him. He knew how nervous she was.

'Do you have milk and sugar in your tea?' Mary asked.

'Milk and one sugar, please,' Jo said. She yearned for a cigarette, but there were no ashtrays.

Anna bounced up and down on her chair. 'Is there any lemonade, Grandma?

Mary put her hand to her mouth. 'Goodness me, I almost forgot.'

Anna giggled.

Mary got the lemonade out of the fridge and poured some into a glass for Anna, then she made the tea and poured it into mugs. At home, Jo's mother would have brought out the best cups, saucers and plates. Here, the plates didn't match and one of them had a chip.

Mary put the mugs on the table and waved a hand towards the butterfly cakes. 'Have a cake. They're just out of the oven.'

Jo helped herself to a cake and bit into it. The filling was lemon curd, her favourite.

Mary sat down and looked at Anna. 'Daddy told me you're going to the zoo.'

Anna scrunched up her face. 'I don't want to see the snakes.'

'They can't hurt you,' Ian said. 'They're behind glass.'

'I don't like looking at them.'

'I'm not going to force you,' Ian said. 'You can look at whatever animals you like.'

Mary stirred her tea. 'I'm sorry if I sound nosy, but how did you and Jo meet?'

Ian squeezed Jo's hand. 'At work. I thought she was the most beautiful girl I've ever seen. And one day I took Anna to the ice rink, and Jo was there, and I thought, what an amazing coincidence, and I asked her out.'

'She can't skate,' Anna said, munching on a cake.

Mary looked at Jo. 'Was it a coincidence?'

Jo's face warmed. 'My friend Ruth heard him talking about it, so we decided to go.'

Ian grinned. 'You didn't twig I did it deliberately.'

'He's joking,' Mary said. 'He was a real prankster when he was little.'

'No, Mum, don't start telling her about that,' Ian said.

Anna pushed back her chair. 'Grandma, can I go play?'

'Course you can, love.'

Mary watched Anna dart out of the kitchen. 'She's a lovely girl,' she said. 'Bit of a worrier, but that's to be expected with the divorce. Still, I can't talk. Ian's father and I separated years ago.'

Ian frowned. 'No, Mum, he walked out and never came back.'

'That's true,' Mary said. 'But I don't like to dwell on it. After Col left, Ian and Trish helped. Trish had just started working, so she gave me board, and when Ian was older he got a paper round.'

'Fighting off mad dogs and bullies,' Ian said. 'Luckily, Billy taught me how to box.'

'Billy's been my neighbour for years,' Mary said. 'Doesn't drink much, and respects women. Lost his wife to cancer a couple of years back. It was very sad. They were devoted to each other. It was a shame they had no kids. At least he's got his dog and his allotment.'

Anna appeared in the doorway. 'I can't find Lucky.'

'Have you looked in his favourite places?' Mary asked.

Anna nodded.

'We'd better go soon,' Ian said. 'We've got the trip to the zoo.'

'I have to pat Lucky before we go,' Anna said.

Mary stood up. 'Alright, let's go find him.'

After she'd gone, Ian picked up Jo's hand and squeezed it. 'See? She doesn't bite.'

'She's kind,' Jo said. 'You're so lucky.'

The expression on Ian's face changed to something like regret. 'Yes, I am,' he said.

...

When they arrived at the zoo, Ian said to Anna, 'What do you want to see?'

'The elephants,' Anna said.

'I like them too,' Jo said.

Anna said nothing.

Jo bit her lip. How was she supposed to get through the weekend with a kid that didn't talk to her?

They walked through the zoo looking at lions and tigers, giraffes and zebras, and Anna talked to Ian but ignored Jo, who wondered if it was because Anna was shy, or she didn't want her there.

A couple of times Ian squeezed Jo's hand. 'Are you alright?' he asked.

She nodded. 'I'm fine.' She felt wounded, stabbed to the heart by a seven-year-old.

At lunchtime, they went to the cafe. Anna finished her chips and stared longingly at Ian's half eaten hamburger. 'Can I have a hamburger, Daddy?'

Ian turned and looked at the long queue. 'You said you didn't want one.'

'I want one now.'

'You can have some of mine.'

Anna shook her head. 'I want one for myself.'

Ian pushed back his chair.

Anna jumped up. 'I'm coming too.'

'Stay with Jo.'

Anna's mouth trembled. 'No, Daddy, I want to come with you.'

Ian gave Jo an exasperated look.

Jo lit a cigarette. Anna was a spoilt little brat. The weekend was a disaster.

When Ian and Anna came back, Anna ate about a third of the hamburger and left the rest.

'You said you wanted it,' Ian said, a hint of annoyance in his voice.

Anna stared down at her plate. 'I'm not hungry.' A tear ran down her face.

In an instant, Jo's resentment vanished. Anna was just a little girl who only saw her daddy every second weekend.

On the table lay some paper serviettes. Jo picked one up and began folding it into the shape of a bird.

After a moment, Anna asked, 'What are you making?'

'A bird,' Jo said. 'It's a crane.' She held it out to Anna. 'It's a bit floppy 'cause it's not the right paper.'

Anna took the bird. 'It's lovely.'

Ian looked at Jo. 'How did you learn origami?'

'From a book,' she said. 'The birds are so beautiful I wanted to make them.'

'You're fantastic.' Putting his arm around Anna, he said, 'I'm sorry for being grumpy, sweetie.'

Anna looked up at him. 'It's alright, Daddy.'

...

Just before bedtime, Ian read Anna a chapter from *Five on a Treasure Island*. 'She can read it herself,' he said to Jo, 'but I like reading to her.'

After Ian finished the story Anna went to bed, asking Ian to leave the door a little open so she could see the living room light. A few minutes later, Ian peered in and gave Jo the thumbs up sign. He came back to the couch and sat down next to Jo.

She picked up one of his hands and turned it over. 'I didn't know you could box.'

'I know how to look after myself,' he said.

She liked that about him. It made her feel safe.

...

Jo woke up in the night, her heart pounding. Anna's screams ripped through the flat. Ian jumped out of bed and pulled on a pair of underpants, then headed towards Anna's room. Jo sat up, pulling the covers around her naked body. She could hear Anna sobbing. Jo got out of bed, wrapped a blanket around herself and crept to the door. Light spilled from Anna's bedroom across the living room. Ian was sitting on the bed, his arms around her. 'There's no tigers here,' he said. 'They live at the zoo. Everything's fine. You can go back to sleep.'

'Can I sleep with you and Jo?' Anna asked.

'You've got your own bed,' Ian said.

'But I want to sleep with you and Jo.'

'How about I make up a bed on the couch,' Ian said. 'We'll be right next door. You'll be able to hear me snoring.' He snorted a couple of times. 'Do you reckon you can sleep listening to that?'

Silence, then, 'Alright,' Anna said in a disappointed voice.

Jo sneaked back to bed. Who would have thought Anna would have a nightmare after a day at the zoo? Looking after kids was harder than she'd thought.

When Ian came back to bed, he said, 'she's gone to sleep.'

'Does she normally have nightmares?' Jo asked.

'Sometimes,' Ian said.

It was clear he didn't want to talk about it.

Jo rolled over and closed her eyes. Today she'd seen parts of Ian she hadn't noticed before, his stoniness when he was angry, his tendency to not talk about things that bothered him. But everyone had a side they didn't like people to see. She was too sensitive, too unsure, a girl who loved nature and books but also clothes and music and dancing. How did you fit those pieces of yourself together into a comfortable whole? Maybe it was a sign of being grown up when you could.

Chapter Fourteen

Jo stood in Ian's bathroom staring into the mirror. Her skin was clear, and the silver straps of her purple dress glittered. The dress was new, bought for the party tonight, which was being thrown by Rick, one of Ian's friends. She was dreading it. When she walked into the living room Ian said, 'You look fantastic.'

She gave him a tiny smile. 'Thanks.'

In the car her hand shook as she pulled out her cigarettes from her fake Glomesh bag.

'You don't have to be nervous,' Ian said. 'Everyone will like you.'

Jo lit up and inhaled. The men might like her but what about the wives? They probably all knew Ange. Some might still be friends with her.

Half an hour later, Ian pulled up behind a line of cars parked in front of a white wooden house in Oakleigh. Lights blazed from the porch and the sound of music came from inside.

Jo shivered as they walked up the path. It was a cold, clear night. Overhead the sky sparkled with stars. Ian knocked on the front door. A minute or so later it opened and a tall man holding a glass of beer stood in the doorway. He opened the door wider. 'Come in.'

'Rick, this is Jo,' Ian said.

Rick smiled. 'Hello, Jo.'

She recognised the look in his eyes. *You're pretty.* She smiled back. 'Hello.'

They went from the hall through a couple of glass doors into the living room, which was L-shaped and smelt of cigarette smoke. The people in the room were all older than Jo. 'Memphis Tennessee' played on the gramophone. Ian handed Rick a bottle of Barossa Pearl and a bottle of red wine. Jo had asked Ian to bring the Barossa Pearl. Drinking wine would make her look more sophisticated.

Rick vanished into the kitchen as a tall blonde woman came over. Her hair was swept up into a French roll and she wore a black shift with a fringe at the hem. She kissed Ian on the cheek. 'Hello Ian, lovely to see you. It's been too long.' She had a German accent like Christina, the new woman at work.

'It has,' Ian said. 'Ingrid, Jo.'

Ingrid smiled. 'I'm glad you could come. I'm Rick's wife. Come and put your coat on our bed.'

Jo followed her through the double glass doors into the hall. A bedroom was on the right, dimly lit.

Ingrid waved a hand at the bed. 'Just put your coat there. The bathroom and toilet are at the end of the hall.'

Jo slipped off her coat and laid it on the bed, then followed Ingrid to the living room, where Ian stood talking with some of his mates. Someone must have told a joke; there was a burst of laughter.

'Would you like a drink?' Ingrid asked.

'A wine, please.' Jo sat down on the nearest chair and lit a cigarette. Her dress belonged in a disco, not here. Ian wasn't looking in her direction. Had he forgotten her already?

Rick appeared with a glass of wine. 'Here, lovely lady, drink up.'

He gave Jo the glass and she raised it to her lips. Across the room two women standing together were eyeballing her. One of them wore a low-cut green dress with a tight waist and flared skirt. The woman's face was perfectly made up, her mahogany-coloured hair back-combed high. The other was smaller and plainer. Jo gulped some wine.

'Hello.'

A short woman with rosy cheeks had sat down next to her. The woman held a plump baby wearing blue flannelette pyjamas.

'I'm Helen,' the woman said. 'This is Timothy.'

'Jo.'

The baby stretched out a dimpled hand and touched Jo's face.

'He likes you,' Helen said.

'How old is he?' Jo asked.

'Nine months. I've got two older ones at home. But I'm sure you don't want to hear about my kids. Tell me about you.'

Sweat broke out under Jo's fringe. What could she say about herself? That she liked reading, rock pools and dancing? Or The Stones in concert at St Kilda? 'I work with Ian,' she said.

'What do you do?'

'I'm an accounts clerk.' Once she'd dreamed of sailing to Hawaii.

'I used to be a draftswoman,' Helen said. 'But I had to leave after I got pregnant with Mark. He's my eldest. People at work feel uncomfortable if you've got a big belly.'

No woman at Jo's work had ever stayed past three or four months of their pregnancy. They turned up months later with their babies for the girls to ooh and ah over and disappeared back to their homes.

'Looking after babies and young children is so *boring*,' Helen said. 'If I hadn't joined the library my brain would be dead by now.'

Weren't marriage and motherhood supposed to be fulfilling?

Timothy arched his back, grizzling.

'He needs his bottle,' Helen said. 'I'd better go and heat it up. Excuse me.'

As she stood up, Ian came over. 'Sorry, sweetheart, I've been neglecting you. Let's get some food.' He took Jo's hand and led her to the table. A cob filled with creamy dip sat in the middle, there were bowls of frankfurters with dishes of tomato sauce, devils on horseback and a platter of mixed cold meats, sausage and cheeses. Ian handed Jo a plate. She picked up some cubes of cheese and a couple of slices of sausage. After Ian loaded his plate, they sat on dining chairs against the wall. Jo took another swig of wine.

'Here,' Ian said, handing her a sandwich cut into small triangles.

Jo bit into the sandwich. Asparagus. The woman in the green dress was eyeballing her again.

'Who's that woman in the green dress?' Jo asked. 'She keeps looking at me.'

'Marcia,' Ian said. 'Ignore her.'

'You don't have to say you love me' played on the gramophone.

Ian stared into his glass of wine. 'What's the matter?' she asked.

'Nothing,' Ian said. He raised the glass to his lips and swallowed.

Jo felt an urgent need to pee. *It must be the wine.* 'Excuse me,' she said, and headed towards the glass doors that led into the hall. The toilet was through a sliding door from the bathroom. When Jo came out, the woman in the green dress stood in front of the mirror. She opened her handbag and took out a bottle of perfume. 'Hello, I'm Marcia.'

Close up, Jo could see the thickness of Marcia's make-up, her pencilled eyebrows.

'Jo,' she said.

'Where did you get your dress from?' Marcia asked. 'It's gorgeous.'

Jo pulled out her hairbrush. 'Thanks. A boutique in the city.' She'd bought it from the South Melbourne Market.

Marcia sprayed perfume under her ears and the bathroom filled with a scent that smelt heavy and cloying. 'It wouldn't matter what you wore. You'd look good in a sack. Ian's always had excellent taste in women. Ange is gorgeous.'

Jo's hairbrush stopped in mid-air.

'You do know about Ange, don't you?' Marcia asked.

Jo nodded.

'Did he tell you the reason why they're divorced?'

Jo brushed her hair with quick, hard strokes. 'I'm not interested.'

Marcia's eyes bored into her. 'He had an affair.'

Jo felt a wave of nausea as she dropped her hairbrush into her bag and walked out.

...

Ian spotted Jo as she came through the double glass doors. Her face was white. He hurried over to her. 'Are you alright?'

'No,' she said in a low voice.

He led her to a couple of chairs in the corner. The Seekers song 'I'll never find another you' filled the room.

'Are you feeling sick?' he asked.

She stared at him as if he was a stranger. 'Marcia was in the bathroom. She told me why you're divorced.'

His belly dropped. Taking her hand he said, 'Let's go outside.'

He led her through the empty kitchen and laundry into the backyard, where a crazy paving patio and coloured concrete tubs edged the lawn. Taking off his jacket, he draped it around her bare shoulders. 'I'm sorry you had to find out like this,' he said. 'I've been a bloody idiot. I should have told you.'

He watched Jo take out her cigarettes and light up, blowing smoke into the chill night air.

'If you're worried about me going out with other women, it won't happen,' he said. 'I meant it when I said I'd try my best to make you happy.'

She was shivering.

'How about we talk in the car?' he asked.

'I need my coat,' she said. 'I want to go home.'

His insides sank. 'I'll get it for you. Will you wait by the car?'

She nodded.

Rick's house had a side gate opening into the front garden. Ian opened it. 'I won't be long,' he said.

She slipped through without a word.

...

Ian went back to the house. He should have known Marcia would do something. She'd tried to come onto him after his divorce, but he'd turned her down. She wasn't the type to forget.

Ingrid stood in the kitchen, cutting up a black forest cake.

'I need Jo's coat,' he said. 'Marcia told her about my divorce. She's upset. I'm taking her home.'

Ingrid made a sympathetic face. 'What a horrible thing to do. She's the one who should be going home.' She wrapped a couple of slices of cake in paper napkins and gave them to him, then went to fetch Jo's coat.

When he got back to the car, Jo stood waiting. He felt relieved she hadn't run off into the dark. They got into the car. He put the pieces of cake in the glove box and started the engine. She sat as far away from him as possible. He wondered if it would be the last time she'd be in his car. They drove to Footscray in silence, while she smoked three cigarettes in a row.

He parked in a street not far from Ruth's place. Lights gleamed from some of the houses, and a dog barked from a backyard. Jo wound down her window and cold air streamed into the car.

'I'm sorry,' he said again.

Jo glared at him. 'Marcia *enjoyed* telling me. If I'd known, I would have been prepared.'

'I didn't want to tell you because I'm not proud of myself,' he said.

Her face was expressionless. 'Tell me now.'

His fingers drummed on the steering wheel. 'Ange and I were twenty when we got married,' he said. 'She was four months pregnant. After the ceremony, we were standing on the steps of the church when the priest rushed out with the marriage certificate. I hadn't signed it. I had this crazy urge to run away, but I was going to be a father. So, I signed.' He sneaked a look at Jo. She was staring through the windscreen.

'Before I got married, I was saving to go overseas, but the money went into a bond for our flat, and things for the baby. After Ange left work, I had two jobs, one in an office and the other at a service station.' An image of the blonde woman he'd screwed behind the service station one night came into his head. He batted it away. 'We didn't see each other much, and it suited me. Ange hated being pregnant, and I wasn't sure how I felt about the baby. Everything was happening too fast. But the first time I saw Anna I had the most amazing feeling of love. I knew I'd kill to protect her. Ange said we should buy a house, and her parents would help. She got a part-time job and her mother minded Anna. I still worked at my two jobs. After a year, we'd saved enough to put down a deposit. Ange wanted to pay off the house quickly, so she got a full-time job. She started going out on girls' nights with friends from work. I wasn't sure if she was seeing other men, but I was depressed and lonely. I had an affair with a girl who worked at the service station.' He sneaked another glance at Jo.

She was sitting, still as a statue. He wondered if she'd heard anything he'd said.

'When Ange found out about Natalie, she told me to leave,' he continued. 'We separated, then Natalie and I split. Ange wanted a divorce. She promised me if we got one I could see Anna as much as I liked, but I had to be the one who admitted to adultery. Afterwards she broke her promise. I can only see Anna once a fortnight and half the school holidays.'

'I feel so humiliated,' Jo said. 'Everyone at that party knew about your divorce except me.'

Ian shrugged. 'I barely see those people. After my divorce, most of my mates' wives didn't want a bar of me. I reckon they thought divorce might be catching.'

'I'm hungry,' Jo said.

He stared at her in surprise. How could she think of her stomach at a time like this? Didn't she realise how gut-wrenching it had been for him to tell her?

'I swear I've been listening,' she said. 'But I'm starving. I've hardly eaten a thing all day.'

Ian leaned towards the glove box and took out the wrapped pieces of cake. 'Black forest cake,' he said.

She took the pieces from him. 'Thanks.'

He watched her wolf them down. 'You've got cream on the end of your nose,' he said.

Startled, she put her finger to her nose and licked it. 'I'm such a dork.'

He looked at her short purple dress under her unbuttoned coat, the length of her legs, her shiny black shoes with rounded toes and narrow ankle straps.

'No, you're a beautiful, sexy, young woman, and I'm nuts about you.' He risked putting a hand on her thigh. She didn't move away. 'Are you feeling better now?'

She nodded.

Relief flooded through him. 'Do you still want to go home?'

'No,' she said. 'Your place.'

Chapter Fifteen

Pale light edged the venetians in Ian's bedroom. Jo could just see the dark shapes of their clothes lying on the floor. Ian slept next to her, breathing quietly. She sat up. The air felt icy. Shivering, she pulled off one of the blankets and wrapped it around her naked body, then picked up her handbag and went into the kitchen. The bare branches of the tree outside made a pattern against the lightening sky and a couple of lights shone from the flats over the road. Switching on the jug, she made tea then went into the living room and turned on the electric heater. The smell of warm dust filled her nose as she crouched in front and lit a cigarette. She wished she'd thought of something clever to say to Marcia instead of showing how shocked she was. Like *What's the matter, Marcia? Pissed off because you wanted him yourself?*

Jo blew out smoke. Ian was so keen on her being honest, she'd assumed he was too. It gave her a sick feeling to think of him lying. How could she trust him anymore?

...

Ian woke and rolled over, saw a line of light under the bedroom door. He put his hand on the other side of the bed. It felt cold. His chest hollowed out. Had Jo gone and left a goodbye note on the kitchen table? He threw back the covers, noticed that a blanket was missing, got up and pulled on underpants, pants and a warm jumper. Opening the bedroom door, he spotted Jo wrapped in the missing blanket sitting on the floor in front of the heater. The look in her eyes reminded him of an abandoned puppy he'd once found on a railway station and taken home. He bounded over and kissed her, injected a playful note into his voice. 'Let's eat, sweetheart. We're going to the city.'

She looked up at I. 'What for?'

'It's a surprise.'

Her mournful face lit up. 'What?'

'Wait 'n' see.'

He'd lain awake last night after Jo had fallen asleep, inhaling the smell of her skin. Everything about her turned him on, that sulky-looking bottom lip, the angle of her hips, the rosy nipples on her breasts. Was she as forgiving as she seemed, or would she be like Ange, dredging up his past mistakes in every future argument? He'd try and make it up to her, buy her something expensive. It would mean paying his rent a bit late, but what the hell. She needed to know how sorry he was.

After Jo dressed and they'd eaten breakfast, they caught the tram into the city and walked down Little Collins Street to the Royal Arcade, where Catanach's Jewellers stood on the corner. Ian stopped and scanned the window, then pointed to a collection of gold and silver watches resting on black velvet pads. 'What do you think of those?'

Jo gaped at the watches. 'They're lovely.'

'Would you like one?' he asked. 'Forget about the money. Just choose.'

She turned and stared at him. 'Really?'

'Yes.' He drank in the intent expression on her face as she stared at the watches. At last, she pointed at a gold one with a round dial and a black leather strap. 'I like that.'

'So do I,' he said. 'Let's go in.'

They entered the shop, which felt hushed and expensive, with thick carpet underfoot and a blaze of lights over glass cabinets.

A thin young man with a droopy moustache came over to them and smiled. 'How can I help you?'

'There's a gold lady's watch with a black strap in the window,' Ian said, 'second row, third from the left.'

The young man went to the back of the window, unlocked it, and brought back the watch. Jo held out her wrist and the young man did up the band.

'What do you think?' Ian asked, admiring the watch on her slender wrist.

Jo's eyes shone. 'It's gorgeous.'

'We'll take it,' Ian said.

'Good choice,' the young man said.

Ian and the young man went to the cash register. Ian took out his wallet and counted out the money.

He took Jo's hand as they left the shop.

Jo looked up at him, her face glowing. 'Thank you. I love it.'

He felt a glow of pleasure. 'I wanted to show you how much you mean to me.'

Her expression changed. 'Are you saying you love me?'

His heart sank. Love led to engagement and wedding rings. He looked down into her face. 'Yes, I love you,' he said. 'But don't start thinking about getting married.'

'I'll always love you,' she said quietly.

He gave a tiny smile. 'You're very young.'

Her face lit up. 'Let's forget about all this and have a perfect day.'

He grinned. 'Alright.' With her it might be possible.

...

At Ruth's place, Jo peeled potatoes and carrots while Ruth browned pieces of lamb in a pot.

'I love your watch,' Ruth said. 'It must have cost a lot.'

Jo glanced at her wrist. 'I don't know how much it cost. The tag was turned over. After we bought it, he told me he loved me.'

'Ooh,' Ruth said. 'When are you getting engaged?'

Jo chopped the peeled carrots. 'We're not.'

Ruth stared at her. 'What will you do? Live together? Hardly anyone does that.'

'Moira and Ollie do,' Jo said.

Ruth tipped chopped onion into the pot. 'They're different.'

'Why?' Jo asked. 'Because they're old? Do you think they do it?'

Ruth shrugged. 'I don't know.'

'I reckon they do,' Jo said. 'I saw them once, holding hands.' They looked so—'

'Cute?' Ruth said.

They giggled.

'My cousin Jane got married when she was eighteen,' Ruth said. 'She was pregnant with twins. Imagine, washing two lots of nappies.'

Jo's nose wrinkled. 'Disgusting.'

'I've just realised I don't know anyone who's happily married,' Ruth said.

Jo handed the plate of carrots to Ruth. 'Susie and Jim are.'

'They've only been married a year. When was the last time you saw your mum and dad kiss each other?'

'Can't remember.'

'Imagine *them* doing it,' Ruth said as she tipped the carrots into the pot.

Jo began chopping the potatoes. 'They probably don't anymore.'

'I hope I don't end up looking like my mum,' Ruth said. 'That'd be the end.'

'At least your mum doesn't have a go at you about how you look.' Jo put on her mum's voice. 'I don't know why you always look so *cheap*, Josephine.'

Ruth snorted with laughter. 'Seriously,' she said. 'Would you live with Ian if he asked you?'

'Yes,' Jo said.

'You're so brave. Don't you care what people think?'

'No,' Jo said. She wished it was true.

...

One lunchtime the following week, Jo got a call from her dad.

'How are you, love?' he asked.

Jo swallowed a lump in her throat. 'I'm fine. How are you?'

'Fine. I just want you to know you'll always be part of this family,' Kev said.

Jo felt a flood of warmth. 'Thanks, Dad.'

'It's your mother's birthday next month. Will you come to her lunch?'

'What about Ian?' Jo asked.

'That might be stretching it. Maybe Christmas.'

'Ian sees his daughter at Christmas. Would she be welcome too?'

Kev sighed. 'What's the world coming to when you ask me if a child will be welcome in my home?'

'She's seven,' Jo said.

'I feel ashamed, and that's the truth.'

'It's not your fault.'

'Your mother wasn't always the way she is now,' Kev said. 'She used to be a smiley girl. You should have seen her on the dance floor. All the boys wanted to go out with her.'

It was hard to believe.

'I'd better get back to work,' Kev said. 'Think about it, love.'

The next day, Maureen called. 'I'm sorry I blamed you,' she said. 'I was feeling stressed about the wedding.' For once, she sounded less sure of herself. 'You do want to be in it, don't you?'

'Course, I do,' Jo said. Why should she miss out? It was the biggest thing to happen in her family for years.

The next time Maureen rang, she said with a triumphant note in her voice that everything was settled, that she'd told their mum that Jo was going to be her bridesmaid and that was that, and their mum had said, 'If it's what you want,' and it was done. 'I was surprised,' Maureen said. 'I expected a battle.'

...

The next morning when Jo and Ruth went into work, Christina stood at the mirror in the girls' room, pencilling her eyebrows into high arches. Christina was close to Nola's age, but she was nothing like Nola. Christina wore clothes that showed off her rounded breasts, although her skirts were longer, hiding her knees. 'Older women do not show their knees,' she'd said, casting an envious glance at Jo's legs. Christina had told Jo that when she first arrived in Australia and was learning to speak English, her boyfriend taught her a lot of dirty words.

'I didn't know what they meant,' she said. 'I felt bad when I found out.'

Christina had also told Jo and Ruth that her current boyfriend was no good. 'He doesn't like dancing,' she said, 'but I love it.' As she said this, she did a little twirl so that her skirt flared out. Over in his glass cubicle Mr O'Shaughnessy stared at her.

Christina frowned as she smoothed her skirt over her thighs. 'That man sees everything.'

She said that any man over twenty-five who wasn't married was a creep, which was why she went out with married men, 'just for a bit of fun'. She said this quietly one day, while she and Jo were standing at the filing cabinets.

Christina looked up her horoscope in *The Sun* every morning and read them out at teatime. *For those who don't have a romantic partner, you're going to meet someone special. Love beckons with the promise of an exciting future.* Sometimes she read the words wrongly. Once Nola tried to correct her, but Christina glared at her and said, 'Don't say this to me like I am a little girl. I am more woman than you.'

Christina had asked Jo what her star sign was.

'Libra,' Jo said.

Christina nodded. 'I guessed. Libras are all about sex.'

Jo slid her coat off and hung it on the rack, then held out her wrist. 'Look what Ian bought me.'

Christina stared at the watch, then Jo. 'He cares about you. Give me your hand.'

Jo held out her hand and Christina turned it over, peering at her palm.

'You're going to have a long life,' she said, tracing a line in Jo's palm. 'See how long it is? Now I see your love line.'

Jo snatched her hand back. 'No.'

Christina looked at her pityingly. 'You are afraid your love affair will end. I tell you this. The ones you love the most are the ones who get away.'

Jo's stomach dropped.

Susie walked in. 'Good morning,' she said brightly. 'How's everyone today?'

'Fine,' Jo said, as she went out into the office.

Ruth followed her. 'Christina's an old witch,' she said quietly. 'Don't take any notice of her.'

Later, when Christina was out of the office, Susie beckoned Jo over. 'What did Christina say to you? You were as white as a sheet.'

'It was nothing,' Jo said.

'You looked really upset.'

Jo shrugged. 'She wanted to read my palm, but I wouldn't let her.'

'Quite right,' Susie said. 'It's a load of rubbish. But you still haven't told me why she upset you.'

'She said I was scared Ian would leave me, and the ones you love the most are the ones who get away.'

'Rubbish,' Susie said. 'Jim's the love of my life and we're married.'

Susie had been twenty-four when she met Jim. He was English and on a working holiday. They were saving to visit Jim's family in London and might stay for a couple of years. Other than that, they had no plans. Jo liked the freedom of it.

Chapter Sixteen

Jo waited near the steps at Flinders Street Station, her foot tapping on the tiled floor. Maureen and Kathleen should be arriving in a couple of minutes. They were going shopping for their wedding clothes, but Maureen was picky and Kathleen impatient. They could easily end up arguing.

At last, Jo spotted Maureen and Kathleen coming through the ticket barriers, Maureen in her beige coat with the faux fur collar, and Kathleen in matter-of-fact navy.

'We're going to visit every bridal shop in Melbourne,' Maureen said as they clattered down the steps.

Kathleen shot Jo a look. *Not a chance.*

Outside, trams rattled across the intersection and the cold nipped at their fingers. They crossed Flinders Street and hurried along the pavement. There were three bridal shops in Swanston Street, before you got to the town hall. Female mannequins with tiny waists and smug faces stood in the shop windows, with child mannequins in front. The child mannequins looked angelic, but Maureen's flower girl was bratty Simone, Michael's niece. Luckily, Simone's grandma was making her dress, so she hadn't needed to come.

The first bridal shop stood at the mouth of a musty arcade with a dingy tiled floor. Long racks of tightly packed dresses lined the walls. At the back stood three changing rooms, curtains neatly hooked to one side. A thin woman dressed in black dashed out to greet them.

'Here comes the first vulture,' Kathleen said quietly.

The woman gave a thin-lipped smile. 'Hello, girls. Who's the lovely bride?'

'I am,' Maureen said.

The woman looked at Jo and Kathleen. 'And you two are the brides-maids. Sisters, aren't you?'

'They're my younger sisters,' Maureen said.

The woman turned to her. 'I've got a new wedding dress that only came in ten minutes ago. Let me show it to you.'

She darted to the back of the shop, returning with a wedding dress in a long plastic cover. Quickly, she unzipped the cover and slid it off. The dress shimmered in the lights. 'It's crystal organza,' the woman said in a hushed voice. 'See that lovely sheen? The appliqued lace on the bodice is exquisite.'

Maureen stared at the dress.

'The ivory will suit your skin tone better than white,' the woman said. 'Why don't you try it on?'

'Yes,' Maureen said.

The woman scuttled towards one of the changing rooms, the wedding dress folded over her arm. Maureen followed.

Jo and Kathleen moved towards the nearest rack of dresses, grouped in pastel shades of pink, blue, aqua and lemon.

At the back of the shop, the woman hung up the dress in a changing room. 'Let me know when you want me to zip you up.' she said, as Maureen went inside. The woman pulled the curtain across and rushed back to Jo and Kathleen.

'What colour are you looking for?'

Maureen's voice came from the changing room. 'Aqua.'

The woman's bony fingers worked at top speed through the aqua dresses on the rack before she pulled one out. 'This is our bestseller.'

'Too fussy,' Kathleen said.

'You want something simpler.' The woman hung the dress up and pulled out another. 'What about this one?'

Jo stared at the dress's scooped neck and empire line bodice, trimmed with lace.

'Imagine this with long white gloves and sweet little posies,' the woman said. 'The material's polyester crepe. It flows beautifully over the body.'

'It's nice,' Jo said. 'What do you think, Kath?'

Kathleen shrugged. 'It's alright.'

The woman pulled out another dress in the same style. 'Here's one in your size,' she said to Kathleen. 'Why don't you girls try them on?'

Maureen's voice came from the changing room. 'Can you please zip me up?'

The woman led Jo and Kathleen to the changing rooms, where Jo took off her clothes and stepped into the dress. In the mirror she looked elegant and sophisticated. She couldn't wait for Ian to see her.

The woman's voice came from outside the changing room. 'Would you like some help?'

'Yes, please.' Jo pulled aside the curtain, lifting her hair so the woman could pull up the zip.

'You look lovely,' the woman said. 'Come outside, where we can see you.'

Jo stepped into the shop, where Kathleen stood barefooted on the carpet. In the mirror, the aqua dresses showed off their blue eyes and flattered their pale skin.

'Beautiful,' the woman breathed.

Maureen walked out from the changing room, and Jo almost gasped. The wedding dress shimmered in the light, its fitted bodice showing off Maureen's breasts and small waist, the skirt flaring over her hips to her feet, finishing in a short train.

'You look stunning,' the woman said. 'Wait. You need shoes.' She dashed behind a curtain and emerged with a pair of white shoes.

Maureen slipped them on while the woman went over to a glass cabinet, where she took out a flowered headpiece and veil, embroidered with tiny bows. 'It's a fingertip veil,' the woman said. 'So pretty.' She fitted the headpiece on Maureen's head and draped the veil on top. Stepping back, the woman said, 'Now look at yourself.'

Maureen stared at her reflection.

'You look fantastic,' Jo said.

'You do,' Kathleen added.

Maureen's eyes narrowed as she stared at Kathleen. 'You're not just saying it, are you?'

Kathleen shook her head. 'No.'

'Walk up and down,' the woman said. 'You need to know how the dress feels when you move.'

Maureen walked the length of the shop and turned.

'You look like a princess,' the woman said. 'No-one will be able to take their eyes off you. Stand together and look at yourselves. You all look fabulous.'

The three of them stood in front of the mirror.

Maureen stared at their reflections, then looked at the woman. 'Can we put these dresses on hold for a couple of hours?'

Jo and Kathleen exchanged a glance. *Typical Maureen.*

The woman's face fell. 'I can only give you an hour,' she said. 'This dress will be sold by lunchtime.'

Outside, Maureen urged, 'Come on, we have to hurry.'

Kathleen scowled. 'We'll waste our time for the next hour and when we go back the dresses will be gone.'

'We could walk Melbourne and won't find anything better,' Jo said.

Maureen frowned. 'You don't buy the first dress you try on.'

'You do if it's perfect.'

An hour and a half later, the three of them stood outside Foys.

'You should have bought that dress,' Kathleen said. 'It's probably gone by now.'

'Shut up,' Maureen said. 'Alright, we'll go back.'

At the bridal shop, the same thin woman emerged from behind the curtain at the rear.

'We want to put the wedding dress and the bridesmaids' dresses on layby,' Maureen said.

The woman's expression turned to fake sympathy. 'I'm sorry, but I held the dress for an hour and when you didn't come back—'

Twin spots of red blazed in Maureen's cheeks. 'You *sold* it?'

'I did tell you the dress would be sold by lunchtime, but there'll be no problem in getting you another one. It's a new line.'

'I'll give it a miss,' Maureen said.

'We want the bridesmaid's dresses,' Kathleen said. 'Don't we, Jo?'

'Yes,' Jo said.

Maureen glared at them. 'No, we don't.'

'We do,' Jo said. 'I'm paying for mine, remember?'

'You can't buy the bridesmaids dresses without the wedding dress,' Maureen snapped.

'Girls these days don't try to match their bridesmaids' dresses to the wedding dress. It's more modern,' the woman said.

Maureen bit her lip. 'Alright,' she said at last.

The woman smiled. 'A lovely choice, girls. You were lucky. The other bridesmaids chose pink.' She went over to the racks and pulled out the dresses, hunted for a pair of long plastic covers and hung them behind the counter. 'Layby's twenty-five percent deposit.' She looked at Maureen. 'Please think about ordering that dress. It was perfect on you.'

Outside, Jo said to Maureen, 'You only said no because someone else got that dress first. Who cares if you get the second one?'

'It's not the point,' Maureen said. 'I wanted that one.'

'Well, you should have bought it when you had the chance,' Kathleen said.

Maureen glared at her. 'Maybe I'll have something made. Let's go to Lincraft.'

'Oh God,' Jo groaned.

...

Ian looked up from the TV as Jo came through the door and kicked off her shoes. 'I'm exhausted,' she said, flopping onto the couch. Her mini-skirt rode up her thighs. Christ, she was sexy. He put his hand on her leg.

'Kath and I got our dresses, but Maureen didn't, so we're going again next Saturday,' she said.

Ian raised his eyebrows. 'And if she doesn't find what she wants, you'll go again.'

Jo made a face. 'I have to.'

'You don't,' he said. 'It's part of the crap around weddings. People spend a fortune getting dressed up for just a few hours. Marriage is a legal contract, but people think it's about love. It's crazy. How do you know you're going to love someone for the rest of your life?'

'I think you can,' Jo said.

He looked down at her solemn face and felt an ache of tenderness. She was so young.

'I want you to come to the wedding,' she said. 'There'll be dancing.'

He'd won prizes for ballroom dancing when he was in his teens, but now was not the time to mention it.

'You'll come, won't you?' she asked.

He looked into her pleading eyes. 'I'll think about it.' He had no intention of going.

'Would you like some coffee?' he asked.

'Please.'

They went into the kitchen where Jo sat down, and Ian spooned coffee into the Italian coffee maker.

'I don't want to go to the wedding on my own,' she said.

Ian lit the stove and put the coffee maker on top. 'You won't be. You'll be with your family. Your mother would throw a fit if I went.'

'I thought you didn't care what people thought.'

'I don't, but it will be easier for everyone if I don't go. How much are you spending on this dress?'

Jo wrinkled her nose. 'Forty-five dollars.'

'For a dress you'll never wear again.'

'I could wear it to a ball.'

He knew she was fooling herself. That dress would never be worn again.

...

In the girls' room on Monday morning, Christina said, 'hello sweetie, how was your weekend?'

Jo hung her coat on the rack. 'I went wedding dress shopping with my sisters. I'm one of the bridesmaids.'

'Ah,' Christina said, 'the big dream that every girl wants. And after they're married, their husbands beat them or spend all their money on beer.'

'Not all marriages are like that,' Jo said.

Christina shrugged. 'Some husbands have affairs or visit prostitutes. What do you think happens when men no longer want to sleep with their wives?'

'There *are* good men,' Jo said.

Christina turned and looked at her. 'You should go out with a boy your own age. Older men have problems.'

Divorce. A child he only saw every second weekend.

'I love him,' Jo said.

'That's nice for you, sweetie.'

'Haven't you ever gone out with a good man?' Jo asked.

'Yes,' Christina said. 'He was boring.'

Jo giggled. 'You crack me up.'

'Excuse me?'

'You make me laugh.'

'I see.'

They went out into the office. Christina's desk was at the back, next to the kitchen. Every day she put a waxed paper packet of sandwiches in the fridge. She said her rent was expensive, and she had to feed her two cats. The men in her life came and went, but her cats were family.

Chapter Seventeen

The following Saturday Ian stepped onto the verandah of his mum's house and knocked on the door. Mary appeared a few seconds later. 'Hello, love,' she said.

He stepped inside and kissed her, and they walked down the hall to the kitchen.

'Where's Jo?' Mary asked.

'Shopping,' Ian said.

Mary switched on the jug and got out the biscuit tin while Ian sat down.

'I was surprised when I met her,' Mary said. 'She looks like a teenager.'

'She's eighteen.'

Mary stared at him. 'Isn't she a bit young for you?'

Ian shrugged. 'We get along fine.'

'I hope you're taking precautions.'

Irritated, Ian said, 'Of course.'

Mary made the tea and put the cups on the table.

'Have you met her family?' Mary asked, opening the biscuit tin.

Ian picked up a gingernut. 'Yes.'

'What do they think of the age difference?'

'They're not mad about it.'

'Do they know you're divorced?'

'Yes.'

'You're being very close-mouthed,' Mary said. 'I think there's a lot more going on than you're telling me. Do you love her?'

Ian looked at Mary's worried face. 'Yes.'

'I think she loves you.'

'Yes,' Ian said. *One day Jo would tell him it was over, that she'd fallen in love with a younger man.*

Mary put her hand on his arm. 'I know your marriage to Ange was a disaster, but you were too young. If you and Jo love each other, why shouldn't you marry when she comes of age? Look at Trish. After all that happened to her, she found a decent man to marry.'

Ian said nothing. For years Trish had fallen for bad men that beat her up. She'd finally escaped to Sydney, where she'd met Phil. Now she had a kid, with another on the way. Ian was happy for her, but he didn't want the same. All he needed was Jo.

...

Jo and Maureen sat at a table in the Coles cafeteria. They'd trawled through several bridal shops and hadn't found a dress Maureen liked.

'God, it's hot in here.' Maureen unbuttoned her coat, revealing a red turtleneck and black miniskirt.

'You could have bought that beautiful organza dress,' Jo said. 'It looked fab on you.'

Maureen gave her a venomous stare. 'If you like it so much, you buy it. Except you're not the one getting married, are you?'

Jo pushed aside her apple pie and stood up.

'Where are you going?' Maureen asked.

'Away from you.'

Maureen followed Jo as she flounced into Bourke Street. 'I'm sorry,' she said. 'I'm stressed. Mum's not talking to Dad. She leaves notes for him on the kitchen table. He told her she'd driven you away.'

'It's true,' Jo said.

'Is Ian coming to the wedding?'

'I don't know.'

Maureen's eyes opened wider. 'Haven't you asked?'

'He said he'll think about it.'

'I want him to come.'

'What about Mum?'

Maureen scowled. 'It's my wedding. If I tell her he's coming, that's it.'

Sometimes Maureen reminded Jo of their mum.

'It's Mum's birthday soon,' Maureen continued. 'I reckon if you send her a bunch of flowers, she'd probably ask you to lunch.'

'Dad already asked me,' Jo said. 'I haven't made up my mind.'

Maureen stared at her in surprise. 'It's not like you to be so stubborn. What's the matter?'

'She told me I was no longer her daughter,' Jo said. 'Can you imagine how that made me feel? And she's always going on about me looking cheap. She doesn't say anything like that to you.'

'Your skirts *are* shorter than mine,' Maureen said.

'They're *not*.'

Maureen gave an exaggerated sigh. 'Let's not fight over miniskirts, *please*.'

They turned into Swanston Street. As they walked along the pavement, Maureen hooked her arm through Jo's. 'I'm going to order the organza dress if there isn't one in the shop. It was perfect. And I'll ignore the look on that patronising cow's face when I do it.'

'Fab,' Jo said. 'You're seeing sense at last.'

They looked at each other and smiled.

...

Monica rang Jo on Monday morning.

'Hello, Josephine,' she said in a cool voice. 'Thank you for the flowers. They're lovely.'

Jo gripped the phone. *Bloody Maureen.*

'Maureen says you'd like to come to my birthday lunch on Saturday,' Monica said. 'It starts at twelve. See you then.'

Jo put down the receiver and lit a cigarette. She wished she had the guts to call back and tell her mother she wasn't coming, that it was Maureen who'd bought the flowers, but the image of her dad's kind face appeared in her mind. He'd be so disappointed if she didn't go.

...

On Saturday Ian cooked pancakes for Jo and Anna.

Jo stared down at her plate. 'I'm sorry, I can't eat.'

'You should have something,' he said. 'It'll make you feel better.'

'I'll be sick,' Jo said in a mournful voice.

He felt impatient. *Why the hell had she said yes if she was getting into such a state?*

'You should have said no,' he said.

'I couldn't. I thought of Dad.'

He sighed. Her family was a mess, and she was caught up in the bullshit. There was nothing he could do to help.

...

Several hours later Jo emerged from the Noble Park station and spotted Michael's old FJ standing in the carpark. Maureen wound down the window and waved. Jo hurried over and climbed into the back.

Maureen turned around, strawberry-blonde hair falling over her shoulders. 'Guess what? Father Brady's coming for lunch.'

Jo made a face. Had Mum invited him to give her a talking to, or was she, as Mum always said, overestimating her importance?

They drove past the service station where Michael and John worked, and Maureen said that John had a nice new girlfriend.

'That's good,' Jo said.

'He had a thing for you,' Maureen said. 'But you were going out with that loser Robert.'

Jo leaned against the seat, which gave off a faint whiff of vinyl cleaner. Her stomach lurched. 'What's happening at home?'

'Mum and Dad are talking again,' Maureen said. 'But it's not the same. Dad's more outspoken, and Mum doesn't like it.'

'It's about time,' Michael said. 'She's too used to getting her own way.'

Jo glanced at him in surprise. Maybe Maureen was in for a shock after they married.

Gum trees beside the railway line flashed past. Michael drove into the new housing estate and pulled up outside the house. Jo opened the door of the car and stepped out. The heels of her boots sunk into the boggy ground.

'Make sure you wipe your boots before you go into the house,' Maureen warned.

'As if I'd forget,' Jo said.

They were halfway to the porch when the front door opened, and Kathleen and Rufus appeared.

Jo put her arms around him as he covered her face with licks.

Kathleen grinned. 'Hello, sis.' She wore a pair of stretchy pants and a baggy jumper, her thick wavy hair massed on her shoulders.

'Still going swimming?' Jo asked.

Kathleen's nose wrinkled. 'Not as much. Mid-year exams.'

'Relax. You'll get all As,' Jo said.

She wiped her boots on the mat, and they went inside. The smell of roast lamb drifted down the hall. Everything still looked the same – the yellow pottery elephant on the hall table, the white phone and the gold mirror hanging on the wall. Her old bedroom door stood open. Inside, Maureen's clothes lay on the floor.

They stepped into the kitchen.

'Jo's here,' Maureen announced.

Monica turned. 'I can see that.'

Shadows lay under her eyes.

'Happy birthday,' Jo said.

Monica offered her cheek, eyes averted. Jo kissed it. Her mum smelt of face powder and her favourite lily of the valley perfume. Jo handed her a present, bought from the tiny gift shop on the ground floor of Coates Building.

'Thank you,' Monica said. 'I'll open it after lunch. Go put your coat on your bed.'

'Where's Dad?'

'In the shed. Kathleen, go and get your father, please.'

Jo went into the bedroom and laid her coat on the bed. A knock sounded on the front door. It was probably Father Brady. She felt a stupid instinct to hide, but there was no need. Back at Ian's flat, he'd kissed her as she was about to leave, said, 'I love you.' It was as if he was sending her into battle. She'd not disappoint him.

Footsteps and the sound of voices came down the hall. Father Brady was asking Maureen about the wedding. Jo went over to the dressing table and stared at herself in the mirror. She wore a teal-coloured dress that was halfway up her thighs.

Kathleen appeared in the doorway. 'Come on, Jo, stop hiding. Do you want Mum to set Father Brady onto you in the bedroom?'

Despite herself, Jo giggled. She took a last look at herself and went with Kathleen into the kitchen.

Father Brady stood with Kev and Michael near the window, while Monica, red-faced and wearing an apron, handed platefuls of food to Maureen, who was putting them on the table.

'Hello, Jo, it's nice to see you,' Father Brady said.

He looked old, his body more stooped, the hair on the top of his head thinning.

'Hello, Father,' she said.

Kev put his arms around her. 'Nice to see you, love.'

She felt a warm glow. 'And you, Dad.'

'Kathleen, we need a jug of water and glasses,' Monica said. 'The rest of you, please sit down.'

The table was set to impress, with a white embroidered tablecloth, napkins to match and gleaming cutlery. On the counter, Mum had set out Grandma's bone china cup and saucer set, patterned with yellow roses. To Jo's horror, Father Brady plonked himself next to her. She glanced at her watch. One o'clock. In a couple of hours, she'd be on the train going home.

'That's a nice timepiece,' Father Brady said.

She looked at Father Brady. 'My boyfriend bought it.'

Monica dumped a jug of mint sauce on the table, a disapproving look on her face. 'Father, would you please say grace?'

Jo folded her hands into the prayer position and closed her eyes as Father Brady spoke the old words. They felt calming. Maybe she'd be able to eat lunch.

The meal was her favourite, roast lamb, baked potatoes and pumpkin with green peas, followed by a lemon delicious pudding and whipped cream. Father Brady and her dad talked about the need to do up the old wooden house where Catholic Youth Club was held, and her dad promised to go to a working bee. After the meal, when they'd drunk their tea, Father Brady patted his stomach and said, 'Monica, I really believe you cook the best lunch in Noble Park. I'm sorry, but I'll have to leave. Confession is on this afternoon. Enjoy the rest of the day with your lovely family.'

Monica smiled. 'Thank you, Father.'

Father Brady stood up, his chair scraping the floor. 'Jo, how about you walk with me to my car.'

Jo's stomach felt as if it had dropped to the bottom of a well.

They walked along the hall in silence, and Jo fought against the feeling that Father Brady was a priest, at least fifty, and she was a stupid little girl.

Outside, he said, 'My child, your mother's concerned about the choices you've made. She tells me your boyfriend's divorced and ten years older, and you left home under his influence.'

'I left home because I wanted to,' Jo said.

'Your mother's very upset.'

Jo shrugged. 'I don't know why. She doesn't like anything about me.'

'Your mother's had a difficult life.'

'Well, she shouldn't take it out on me.'

They walked in silence along the path towards the pampas grass at the gate.

'Are you and your boyfriend serious about each other?' Father Brady asked.

Jo nodded. 'Yes, Father.'

'But he's divorced. Did he marry in a Catholic church?'

'Yes.'

Father Brady shook his head. 'Dear me. That's a pity. Marrying in the church means he cannot marry again.'

They'd reached the nature strip. The young tree planted in the middle had lost its leaves; they lay scattered on the grass, small patches of brown and gold.

Father Brady glanced down at Jo's bare knees.

Did he think she was a slut because she slept with Ian?

'It can be very difficult to resist the pleasures of the flesh,' he said. 'Yet the church forbids relations outside marriage. I'd be happy to hear your confession, my child.'

Never.

Father Brady put a hand on her shoulder. 'Please think about it. And God bless you.'

Jo felt a twinge of guilt. Father Brady was kind. She watched him get into his car, easing himself into his seat, turned and went back to the house.

Opening the front door, she went down the hall. Voices came from the kitchen.

'I do hope Father Brady can talk sense into her,' Monica said. 'She's worrying me to death. How could she go against the rules of her faith after all she's been taught?'

Jo walked into the kitchen. 'Why don't you ask me to my face,' she said. 'You might get an answer.'

Kev put a hand on Jo's arm. 'Come on, love. Let's watch your mother open her presents.'

'Not until we've washed up and put everything away,' Monica said.

Jo helped her sisters clear the table while Monica ran water into the sink.

'Mrs Lane is stealing lingerie,' she said in a disapproving voice.

'Yesterday she took a new bra. I kept an eye on the till all day and she didn't pay for it. It's not the first time. I don't know how she gets away with it.'

'She's the manageress,' Kathleen said 'Probably fiddles the books. You should report her.'

'What if I'm wrong?' Monica asked. 'I couldn't work with her after that, and I like my job.'

'What if the staff write a letter,' Kathleen said. 'Then it's not just you.'

Monica shook her head. 'They grumble about her, but they won't do a thing.' She dumped a load of plates into the soapy water. 'I should have taken the manageress job when it was offered to me.'

'Why didn't you?' Kathleen asked.

Monica glanced at Jo. 'Because I always put my family first.'

Jo felt a twinge of irritation. Was her mother trying to make her feel guilty again?

When the kitchen looked spotless, they went into the lounge, where Jo noticed her baby picture sitting on the mantelpiece. Her irritation vanished. She was still part of the family.

Monica smiled when she opened Jo's present, a biscuit barrel shaped like an owl. 'This is nice. Thank you, Jo.'

Jo immediately felt lighter, but it showed how much she wanted her mum's approval.

Just before Jo left, Monica said, 'Does Ruth have a phone number?'

Jo nodded. 'Yes.'

Monica fetched her address book, and Jo wrote the phone number down.

'Give me a hug,' Monica said.

Jo put her arms around her. She felt thin, her skin close to her bones.

'It's been nice to see you,' Monica added.

'And you,' Jo said. *Coming here today was the right thing to do*, she thought.

In Michael's car on the way to the station, Maureen asked, 'What did Father Brady say?'

'He offered me confession,' Jo said. 'And by the way, don't ever do that again.'

'Do what?'

'Buy Mum flowers pretending they're from me.'

Maureen tossed her hair over her shoulder. 'It worked, didn't it?'

'It was dishonest.'

'So, having a sneaky weekend with Ian isn't? I was trying to help. What else did Father Brady say?'

'Not much.'

'Go on. Tell us.'

'He said Ian can't marry me because he was married in a Catholic church.'

'Father Brady's talking rubbish,' Michael said, as he drove into the station carpark. 'You could marry in a registry office.'

It was a thrilling thought.

The next afternoon, Ian pulled up outside Ange's house with Anna. It was five o'clock and the sun was beginning to dip towards the west. The front door of the house opened, and Ange stepped outside. Ian searched her face for clues as she came down the path. Once, in a temper, she'd thrown a full coffee pot at him. She'd missed and the coffee pot hit the kitchen wall, spraying coffee across the plaster. Her temper was almost as bad as his.

He reached over for Anna's bag as Ange walked across the nature strip and yanked open the passenger door.

'Go inside,' she said to Anna. 'I want to talk to your father.'

Anna gave Ian a worried glance, slid out of the car and went slowly up the path.

Ange waited until Anna had gone into the house before she said, 'I've heard you've got a teenage girlfriend. How old is she?'

Ian scowled. Someone from the party, probably Marcia, had told her.

'Eighteen,' he said.

'You're disgusting.'

Ian's eyes narrowed. 'How old's your boyfriend then?'

Ange pouted. 'None of your business.'

'It is,' Ian said. 'He's in my daughter's life.'

'Twenty-two.'

'So, it's alright for you to have a younger boyfriend but not for me to have a younger girlfriend.'

Ange glared at him. 'It's not the same and you know it. She's just a kid.'

'She's very mature.'

'I'm sure she is, thanks to you.'

A wave of fury swept over him. He looked over at the house and spotted Anna's anxious face looking out at them from the lounge room window.

'You'd better watch yourself,' Ange said. 'Go any younger and you'll be in trouble with the law.' She slammed the passenger door and marched towards the house.

Ian started the car and planted his foot on the accelerator. The car roared up the street and screeched around the corner. He was almost in the CBD before he was able to calm down.

Chapter Eighteen

Jo stood in front of her wardrobe. Ian was taking her to Rick and Ingrid's tonight, and she didn't want to go. It had only been a few weeks since the party and the memory of her humiliation was too fresh. She pushed aside the purple dress she'd worn the night of the party and chose a black miniskirt, and a hot pink top with a round collar.

In the car, Ian said, 'Don't worry, sweetheart. Everything will be fine.'

His words made no difference. Jo's stomach churned as she lit a cigarette.

They pulled up outside the house, where a light shone on the porch. Soft rain blew into their faces as they walked to the front door.

Rick opened it and smiled. 'Come in.'

Ian grabbed her hand and squeezed it as they stepped inside.

In the living room a fire burned in the wood heater and white pottery lamps glowed from the sideboard. The table was set for four, with shining cutlery and wine glasses at each place.

Ingrid appeared in a navy dress and cream cardigan with pearl buttons.

'How nice to see you both,' she said. 'Jo, come and put your coat on the bed.'

Jo followed her into the bedroom and took off her coat, aware of Ingrid's eyes on her thin top.

'Don't you feel the cold?' Ingrid asked.

'I'll be fine,' Jo said. 'Your living room's warm.'

'You'd think coming from Germany, I'd be used to the cold,' Ingrid said. 'But Australians don't know how to heat their houses.'

'How long have you been here?' Jo asked.

'Ten years,' Ingrid said. 'It was very hard at first. I was fifteen and missed my friends. At school, the other girls picked on me because of my accent, but things changed when they found out I was good at netball. I used to play for the state. After a couple of years my parents paid for me to go back to Germany for a visit, and I found my old friends had grown up, some of them had gone away, and everything was different. I love Germany, but my life is here.'

'I've never been overseas,' Jo said.

'Go if you can,' Ingrid said. 'It will change your life.'

Jo said nothing. It would take years for her to save the fare. She followed Ingrid into the living room.

'I'll be back soon,' Ingrid said. 'Make yourselves comfortable by the fire. Rick, get them some riesling, please.'

Rick winked at Ian. 'Yes, my love.'

Jo and Ian sat on the couch. He put an arm around her. 'Relax, sweetheart.'

Rick returned with the riesling. He poured it into four glasses and handed one to Jo. She took a sip. The riesling tasted sour, but she gulped some more.

A mouth-watering smell came from the kitchen.

'Ingrid's cooking schnitzels,' Rick said. 'They're her specialty.'

'How are the boys?' Ian asked.

'Asleep,' Rick said. 'Thank God. How's Anna?'

'Good,' Ian said. 'At school, of course.'

'Access going well, then.'

Ian nodded. 'So far.'

Rick looked at Jo, his eyes taking in her face and hair. She'd shampooed it when she'd got home from work, rinsed it in vinegar, for the shine. 'Ian told us you met at work.'

'Yes,' Jo said.

'She sits just outside my cubicle,' Ian said. 'I see her whenever I look up.'

Rick smiled at Jo. 'She must be a hell of a distraction.'

Ian grinned. 'Constantly.'

Ingrid called from the kitchen. 'Rick, I need some help.'

'Sounds like I'm needed,' Rick said. He waved at the table. 'Take a seat.'

Sitting at the table, Jo took another swig of wine. Warmth spread through her veins.

Rick and Ingrid came in, carrying plates of food – golden-coloured schnitzels with a slice of lemon, perfectly fried chips and cucumber salad.

'Ian, mate, you need to shift,' Rick said. 'It won't do for me to sit next to my wife.'

Jo looked at Ingrid. Her face was expressionless.

Rick plonked himself down next to Jo. She caught a whiff of his aftershave, heavy and masculine. He smiled at her. 'Eat up. Don't let it get cold.'

Over the meal, Ian and Rick talked about Holdens and which model they thought was the best and how it compared to the 1965 Falcon, while Jo listened to Ingrid talking about her netball coaching. It was important to get out of the house, Ingrid said, sometimes she felt like a bear in a trap. She said it quietly, so Rick didn't hear.

Jo was surprised. Ingrid had a husband, twin boys and a nice house. Wasn't being married to someone you loved and having his babies enough?

They'd just finished the apple strudel when Rick's hand clamped onto Jo's thigh. She froze. The last time she'd been touched up was in a packed train, just out of Flinders Street. She'd felt soft hands on her body and glanced around. A man stood behind her, looking out of the window. She'd said in a loud voice, 'Stop touching me up.' The man stopped, and at the next station he got off. She'd been so angry. No-one in the carriage had said a word.

'Excuse me.' Getting up, Jo grabbed her handbag and stalked to the bathroom, closing the door. In the mirror her face was pale, her eyes swimming with angry tears. What kind of a bastard touched up his old mate's girlfriend? Why hadn't she said something? She wasn't scared of Rick, but she would feel bad if she made a fuss. It was weird how she could protest in a carriageful of strangers but not here.

A knock came on the bathroom door, and Ingrid's voice said, 'Jo, are you alright?'

Jo took a deep breath, said, 'Yes, I'm fine.' She turned on the taps and water splashed into the pink basin. Behind it were square pink tiles, the grout spotless.

'Can I come in?' Ingrid asked.

'Yes.' Jo wet her hankie and wiped at her smudged mascara as the door opened and Ingrid walked in.

'Something happened with Rick, didn't it?' she said.

Jo's mouth dropped open. 'How did you know?'

'Rick likes pretty girls. When he sat next to you, I knew he was going to do something, but I didn't know how to stop it.'

Jo opened her handbag. 'He put his hand on my thigh.'

'I'm sorry.'

'It's not you who should be sorry,' Jo said.

Ingrid folded her arms. 'I know. And now you wonder how I put up with him. He's a good breadwinner and the father of my boys. My parents are dead, and I have no brothers or sisters. If I leave, my life will be a lot harder, and so will theirs. Look at Ian. He has no money, and he only sees his child every second weekend. I don't want that for my boys. Come back to the table with me. I will sit next to Rick, and you will sit next to Ian, and we'll drink more wine and have a good time.'

Ingrid's blue eyes were steady and calm, willing her to silence.

Jo finished applying more mascara. She would keep quiet, not for Rick but for Ingrid.

'Are you ready?' Ingrid asked.

Jo nodded.

Ingrid linked her arm through Jo's as they left the bathroom.

Chapter Nineteen

As Ian drove towards Elwood, Jo stared through the windscreen. 'Rick gives me the creeps,' she said.

Ian flicked her a glance. 'He was a bit flirty, but you'd be used to that, wouldn't you?'

She felt a surge of anger. Was it his way of saying she looked cheap? 'The lights are turning red,' she said.

Ian slowed down; they came to a stop behind a Ford Falcon.

'Look at that car,' Ian said. 'If I had the cash, I'd buy one tomorrow.'

Jo's nails dug into her palms. She was beside herself and he was talking about bloody cars. 'I don't want to go to their place again,' she said.

Ian looked at her in surprise. 'Why? What's wrong?'

'He put his hand on my thigh.' She watched Ian's face register the shock. 'Jesus. I'm sorry, sweetheart.'

'I should have slapped his face,' Jo said.

Ian whistled. 'That would have been something to see.'

'It's not funny.'

'I didn't say it was.'

Jo lit a cigarette as the lights turned green, and the car moved forward.

'Ingrid knew. She came to the bathroom and talked to me. I couldn't stand to see her humiliated, so I said nothing.'

'You should have,' Ian said.

Jo blew out smoke. 'I'm a Libra. We try and keep the peace.'

'So, you let Ingrid sweet talk you into pretending nothing happened. She can take care of herself.'

Jo frowned. 'Are you saying if you marry a bastard, you get what you deserve?'

'Only if you stay.'

'She's got the twins to think of.'

'Yes, but it's better to live by yourself than with someone who humiliates you.'

Of course, he'd say that. He'd left.

He was looking at her. 'Sweetheart, I promise we'll never go to Rick and Ingrid's again. People who make trouble for us have no place in our lives.'

Her temper flared. 'I hope you're not talking about my family.'

'Only your mother.'

Jo stubbed out her cigarette. 'That's horrible.'

'What's horrible was her saying you're no longer her daughter.'

Jo wound down her window, letting cold air rush in. Those words still hurt.

'Come here,' Ian said.

She wriggled closer to him.

'You can't choose your parents,' Ian said. 'My father's a bastard, and I'll never forgive him.'

She was shocked at the anger in his voice. Although her mum was a pain, she didn't hate her.

...

Jo and Ian waited in the foyer at the Chadstone bowling alley as Maureen and Michael walked through the door. Maureen's blonde hair, now a warm gold colour, fell almost to her breasts, and her black stretchy pants and striped top showed off her curves.

'Let's make it Ian and me against you and Michael,' Maureen said, as they laced up their bowling shoes. 'It'll be fun.'

Jo looked at Ian, who shrugged.

'Fine,' Michael said.

Maureen smiled.

Jo felt a prickle of suspicion. Maureen was up to something.

The game started. Jo sat next to Michael while Maureen bowled. She left two pins standing. When it was Ian's turn, he knocked all ten down.

Maureen clapped her hands. 'A strike. Well done!' She jumped up from her seat and flung her arms around him. The hug lasted a little too long.

Jo turned to Michael, who sat beside her, glum-faced. 'Have you two had a fight?'

Michael shook his head. 'No, but she's been acting a bit weird, lately.'

Jo stared at Ian. Was he enjoying Maureen's flirting? It was hard to tell.

After a couple of games, Ian and Michael went to get the drinks.

Maureen sat down next to Jo. Fishing her compact out of her bag, she opened it and peered at her reflexion.

'Why are you flirting with Ian?' Jo asked in an icy voice.

Maureen snapped her compact shut. 'Don't be stupid. I thought it would be fun to go out in a foursome, that's all.'

'Bullshit.'

Maureen dropped her compact into her bag. 'I'm having doubts,' she said in a low voice.

Jo stared at her in surprise. 'What, about getting married?'

Maureen nodded. 'I always expected to marry Michael, but I've known him for years. You and Ian have got some kind of thing going on. I bet you have a terrific sex life.'

Jo's mouth dropped open. How could Maureen envy *her*?

'You probably think I've got wedding nerves,' Maureen said. She gave a little shrug. 'We're supposed to marry and have kids, aren't we? I'd hate to end up like Auntie Eileen.'

Unmarried and alone. No wonder she hit the bottle now and then.

'Can you put it off for a bit?' Jo asked.

Maureen shook her head. 'The reception's booked, we've ordered the cake and bought the dresses. It's just nerves. I'll be alright.'

Ian and Michael were coming towards them.

'From now on, you play with Michael and I'll play with Ian,' Jo said.

Maureen nodded. 'Alright.'

Later, on their way home, Jo told Ian what Maureen had said.

Ian scowled. 'It's got nothing to do with the wedding. She did it because she's jealous. You should be angry with her, sweetheart. Really bloody angry.'

Sometimes Maureen could be nice, surprising Jo with a sudden hug, a complicit look, occasionally siding with her against their mum. But once, when Jo and Maureen were little, Maureen threw Jo's teddy bear into the toilet and flushed it. Jo screamed as Denny bobbed around in the water. Monica rushed in, told Jo to stop screaming and ordered Maureen to her bedroom. Denny was fished out, taken to the laundry sink and lathered with yellow soap. After Monica had rinsed him, she got an old towel from the linen cupboard.

'Here,' she said, giving the wrapped bear to Jo, 'He needs a cuddle.'

Jo held Denny close to her chest as she heard Monica tell Maureen that she was lucky to have a little sister and had to tell Jo she was sorry. But later, when Jo and Maureen were alone, Maureen gave Jo a Chinese burn, and said if Jo screamed she'd set Denny on fire.

...

At Ian's flat he and Jo had sex, and she fell asleep. Ian lay awake, listening to the occasional car passing in the street below. He didn't like Maureen. She was one of those women who hogged the limelight, so whether she had doubts or not, the wedding would go ahead. There was no way he'd go, even if Jo got down on her knees and begged. It was irritating to see how much she'd been sucked into the wedding-day bullshit. Her face lit up when she talked about her dress, and the satin shoes dyed to match, and the fact that the reception place in the Dandenongs had a parquet dance floor. It was all about the show and nothing about the cold hard reality of living with someone you might end up hating.

His own wedding day had been fraught. Ange looked exquisite but was wound up, while he felt a rising sense of panic. After the reception, held at Ange's parents' place with hordes of her uncles, aunties, cousins, and their kids, and his own tiny family of his mother and Tricia, he and Ange had set out for their honeymoon at Anglesea. As he drove through the dark, something clattered as it hit the road. Pulling up, he checked the outside of the car. One of the hub caps had come off. He was hunting for it in the ditch when Ange wound down the window and told him to just get in the car. He ignored her. By the time he found the hub cap, fitted it, and got back into the car, she was in a sulk. The honeymoon hadn't been great either. When they had sex, he felt uneasy about doing it with the baby inside her. Stupid, maybe, but he couldn't help it. And Ange had morning sickness; most times he woke to the sounds of her spewing in the bathroom.

His mind turned to Rick, hot-shot lover and arsehole. Rick had played the field until he met Ingrid and settled down. But one night, after Ingrid had the twins, Rick came around to Ian's flat. Over a couple of beers, Rick told him that Ingrid had stopped wanting sex, said she was exhausted looking after the twins all day and getting up half the night, but it didn't stop her from throwing Tupperware parties for her friends and coaching the local netball team. Some of the women at his work were looking more attractive by the day. If Ingrid didn't watch out, she'd have something to feel jealous about. Ian had felt some sympathy for Rick, but he felt none for him now.

Jo murmured in her sleep. Ian leaned over, lifted the hair from the back of her neck and kissed the soft skin underneath. Being with her made him feel intensely alive.

...

On Saturday morning, Ian drove to Werribee to pick up Anna. As usual, Martin's grey EH Holden stood in the drive. Ian tooted the horn, and the front door opened. Anna came out and skipped down the path.

Ian leaned across and opened the passenger door. Anna climbed in, leaning forward for his kiss. 'Guess what, Daddy? Mum and Martin are getting married.'

Ian's belly dropped. Could Martin be trusted to take care of Anna? Whether Martin could or not, there was nothing Ian could do. 'That's nice,' he said.

Anna fiddled with her pink plastic bangle, a sure sign she was uncomfortable.

'Mum says Jo's too young for you.'

Ian scowled. 'Jo and I love each other,' he said.

...

While Ian was picking up Anna, Jo wandered around Ian's flat. If she lived here she'd grow plants on the balcony and get rid of his old couch. It was disgusting. He'd told her he'd picked it up from someone's nature strip; she had an awful suspicion that the stain on the front was from a dog lifting its leg. Once she'd bent down to smell the stain, but only a musty odour filled her nose. She went out to the balcony and lit a cigarette. Minutes later, Ian's car swept into the carpark.

When Ian and Anna came inside, Ian's face was expressionless, which meant he was annoyed, or upset, or both.

After Jo and Anna kissed hello, Anna said, 'Guess what? My mum's getting married.'

Jo's eyes widened. Ange had been married to Ian. She'd had his baby. Now she was getting another husband and maybe another baby. Jo forced herself to smile. 'That's lovely. When?'

'November,' Anna said. 'Mum's buying me a lace dress.'

Jo glanced at Ian. His eyes were bleak.

Later, at the park, while Anna climbed to the top of the slide, Jo asked, 'Are you alright?'

'I'm fine,' Ian said.

She stared at the muscle throbbing in his cheek. 'You're not.'

'Leave it, will you?'

She felt as if he'd hit her. 'I'm only trying to help.'

'Well don't.'

She shoved her hands in her pockets. Damn. She'd left her cigarettes at the flat. She stood up.

'Where are you going?' he asked.

'Somewhere else.'

'Don't get in a shit.'

'I'm not.' She was upset. Over Ange getting married, and his refusal to talk to her. 'I just want to be by myself for a bit.'

...

Ian watched Jo as she walked off. Didn't she know he hated talking when he was angry? As her slim form faded into the distance, his anger began to ebb and remorse took over. He lost his temper too easily.

Chapter Twenty

On Sunday evening after Ian dropped Jo at Ruth's, Betty was waiting for her.

'Your mother called,' she said. 'All this time you've been telling me you're going home at weekends. Now I know you've been spending them with your boyfriend. Pack your things. Your father's coming to pick you up.'

The door opened, and Ruth and Carl came in.

'What's happening?' Ruth asked.

'Jo's leaving,' Betty said. 'She's a deceitful little liar. Her father's coming to take her home.'

The bell on the milk bar's door tinkled, and Betty marched out.

Ruth stared at Jo. 'What are you gonna do?'

'I'm not going home.' Jo ran upstairs to her bedroom and flung open the wardrobe door. Pulling her clothes off the hangers, she threw them onto the bed then dragged the old grey suitcase out from underneath.

Ruth appeared in the doorway as Jo flipped open the lid of the suitcase.

'You have to go to Ian's,' Ruth said. 'You can't sleep under a bridge.'

Jo looked up her. 'Will you and Carl take me?'

'Of course, we will.' Ruth clattered downstairs, came back with Carl.

The three of them carried Jo's things down to the living room.

Carl was opening the front door as Betty emerged from the milk bar. 'What are you doing? Jo's father's coming for her.'

'We're taking her to Ian's place,' Ruth said.

Betty stared at Jo. 'If you do this, you're going to regret it for the rest of your life.'

'No, I won't,' Jo said. She bent down to pick up her box of records and carried it outside, where Carl's old car stood at the kerb.

As Carl stowed Jo's things in the boot, Jo glanced at the oncoming traffic. Any one of those cars could be Dad's.

'Let's go,' Carl said.

Jo climbed into the back of the car, pushing aside the green checked rug that smelt of his dog, while Ruth and Carl got into the front. As Carl drove towards Elwood, trams rumbled past and streetlights shone under the bare-limbed trees. Jo felt sick. What would Ian do when she turned up on his doorstep? Where would she go if he didn't take her in?

When they arrived at his block of flats the windows were dark. Jo felt a strange sense of relief. 'He's probably gone to the launderette.'

They carried Jo's things upstairs and heaped them on the landing next to Ian's front door.

'You don't have to wait,' Jo said. 'I'll be alright.'

Ruth and Carl looked at each other. 'Yes, we do,' Ruth said. 'Just until Ian gets here.'

Jo opened her bag and pulled out her cigarettes while Ruth stood by the window that looked down into the carpark. About fifteen minutes later, she said, 'He's back.'

Jo heard the door downstairs open and close. Her heart pounded as Ian's footsteps sounded in the stairwell. He appeared around the corner carrying his basket of clean washing. When he saw her, his expression changed to surprise and something else Jo couldn't name. His eyes flicked across her things. 'What's wrong?'

'My mum threw Jo out,' Ruth said.

'Dad was coming to pick me up,' Jo added.

'This is my boyfriend, Carl,' Ruth said.

Ian nodded. 'Mate.' He unlocked the door. 'You'd better come in.'

Jo bit her lip. It wasn't much of a welcome.

Ian dumped his basket of washing on the couch while Jo's things made a lonely pile on the floor.

Ruth looked at Jo. 'Are you alright, now?'

Jo nodded.

Ruth looked at Ian, then back at Jo. 'Are you sure?'

'Yes,' Jo said. 'And thanks.'

'See you tomorrow.'

After Ruth and Carl had gone, Jo held out her hand. 'You don't want me here. Give me your car keys. I'll sleep in the car.'

'Don't be ridiculous,' Ian said.

Her teeth chattered.

'You're cold,' he said, but he didn't move to touch her.

She sat on the couch next to his basket of washing as he crossed the room and switched on the heater, then he came back and dumped the basket on the floor. She felt the sofa give as his weight settled into it, the warmth of his arm as he put it around her shoulders.

'I'm sorry,' he said. 'This is all a bit sudden.'

'It's only until I find another place,' she said.

He said nothing.

She fought to hold back her tears.

...

Ian carried Jo's suitcase into the bedroom and put it down. She was in a state, and he had no idea what to do. He waved a hand at the wardrobe. 'You can hang your stuff in there.'

'What about a drawer?' she asked.

There were three drawers inside the wardrobe. The first two held his ties, underwear and socks. He pulled out the bottom drawer and froze. A pair of Elaine's silky knickers were inside. *Jesus.* Jo had seen them. She looked stricken. He snatched up the knickers, bunching them into a ball. 'Sorry. They were my ex-girlfriend's. Before your time.'

He went through to the kitchen and dropped the scrunched-up knickers in the bin. Why hadn't he got rid of them before? Jo would think he was a perv who collected women's underwear. But the knickers were nothing compared to the fact that she was here, in his flat, with nowhere to go. They'd only been together for a few months. It was too soon. He wasn't ready.

Jo had followed him into the kitchen, her eyes like those of a puppy waiting to be kicked.

He felt ashamed. 'Sweetheart, I'm sorry,' he said. 'I should have thrown those knickers out.'

'It's my fault,' she said.

He gaped at her. 'What?'

'I lied to Betty every weekend I came here. I said I was going to my parents' place.'

She came over and wrapped her arms around him. He felt as if they'd switched ages, and that she was the older one comforting him.

'I'll make it work,' she said. 'I promise.'

It took two to make things work. He didn't have the heart to tell her.

...

Jo woke to a chorus of birdsong. Next to her Ian lay on his back, asleep. If Mum ever got round to talking to her again, she'd say he'd never marry her now because he'd eaten his cake already. What kind of cake was she, a Victoria sponge with passionfruit icing, light and sweet, or a boiled fruit cake, dark and heavy that sat in your stomach like a stone? Tears slid down her cheeks. Ian would think she had trapped him.

She slid out of bed, picked out some clothes and went into the bathroom. When she came back, Ian was awake. She bent down and kissed him.

He ran a finger down the side of her face. 'I love you,' he said, as if it would make her forget his reaction to her coming, his ex-girlfriend's knickers in his drawer. But she wouldn't.

'Are you gonna eat breakfast?' she asked.

He shook his head. 'Not today.'

She got dressed while he was in the bathroom, then she went into the kitchen. Outside the leafless branches of the old tree loomed dark against the lightening sky. She lit a cigarette and made a cup of instant coffee, dropping in two teaspoonfuls of sugar. A rash prickled on the inside of her wrist, a sign that she was stressed. She'd dreamed of living with Ian one day, but not like this.

...

Ian came out of the bathroom with a towel wrapped around his middle. As he padded through the living room, he spotted Jo sitting at the kitchen table, smoking. He pulled on his clothes and went to the kitchen. Pulling out a chair, he sat down. 'Sweetheart, we need to talk.'

Her hand shook as she stubbed out her cigarette. She looked very young.

'I'll be honest with you,' he said. 'I got a shock when you turned up.'

It had been one of those moments he'd dreaded since childhood, when something unexpected comes out of nowhere, changing your life in an instant. He picked up her hand. 'I do love you.'

Her voice trembled. 'Please don't tell me to leave.'

'Of course, I won't.'

Her face lit up, as if they were going to live happily ever after, like in some fucking fairy tale. He had no idea how he was going to support her, and he hated the idea of her giving him money. And if she thought he'd propose, she'd be disappointed. Turning over her hand he kissed her wrist, avoiding a red patch of rash.

'Don't tell anyone at work we're living together,' he warned. 'People can be nasty. You'll get upset.'

Her face fell. 'Alright, I won't,' she said. 'But I feel like telling everyone.'

He knew he'd ruined her moment of happiness, but she had to grow up sometime. He wondered if her parents would go to the cops, try and get him charged with something. If Ange found out she'd go to court and apply to have his access to Anna stopped. It would break him.

He watched Jo take her coffee cup to the sink. She'd find out that living with him wasn't a bed of roses. He could be irritable and bad-tempered, and he had a past, as his mum liked to say.

...

At work, Jo got a call from Maureen.

'The whole house is in chaos,' Maureen said in a doomsday voice that reminded Jo of their mum.

Outside, a pigeon walked along a window ledge of the building behind, its pink claws gripping the edge.

Maureen's voice came down the line. 'Jo? Are you there?'

'Yes,' Jo said.

'Mum says you can't be my bridesmaid, but I said you were, and I wasn't going to change my mind. That put her back in her box.'

'Thanks, sis. It's fab I'm still in the wedding.' To Jo's surprise, she meant it. 'Are Mum and Dad going to the cops?'

'No,' Maureen said. 'We told them it would make things worse, so Mum went to see Father Brady. He said it was a bad idea. Sorry, I've got a customer. Talk to you later.'

Jo hung up. She got up and went into Ian's cubicle.

He picked up his phone. 'I'm busy,' he said. 'Talk later.'

She went back to her desk, feeling deflated.

Chapter Twenty-one

One lunchtime, when Jo and Ruth were eating their sandwiches, Jenny from the typing pool went into the girls' room and closed the door. She was eighteen and pretty, with curly brown hair and what Christina called 'a nice figure'. Seconds later, the sounds of muffled crying came over the top of the partition.

Susie got up from her desk and went into the girls' room. Jo and the others followed.

Jenny sat on the lumpy couch, tears running down her face. Susie sat next to her, an arm around her shoulders.

'He won't be back for weeks,' Jenny said. 'His ship's just left for Hamburg.'

He was Jimmy, Jenny's Irish boyfriend from Belfast.

'Do you think he'll marry you?' Susie asked.

Jo and Ruth exchanged a look. *She's pregnant.*

'Maybe he got a wife and kids in Belfast,' Christina said.

Susie glared at her. *Shut up.*

'Do your parents know?' Susie asked.

Jenny shook her head. 'I'm too scared to tell them.'

'What about your landlady?'

'No.'

'When he gets back you have to tell him straight away.'

Jenny mopped her eyes with her hankie. 'I know.'

'Try not to worry,' Susie said. She eyed Christina. *Keep quiet.*

Judith's loud voice travelled over the top of the partition. 'I'm sorry, but Mr O'Shaughnessy's stepped out of the office. Can I take a message?'

Jenny pushed her hankie into her sleeve. 'Here's me crying over being pregnant, and she'd be over the moon.'

Christina went out, returning with a small glass jar containing what looked like chopped-up flowers. It was one of the weird teas she drank instead of proper tea with milk and sugar.

'I make camomile tea,' she said. 'It will calm you.'

Jenny cast a suspicious glance at the jar. 'What does it taste like?'

'You don't like the taste, you hold your nose,' Christina said.

'Everything will be fine,' Susie said to Jenny. 'Wait and see.'

...

'Poor Jenny,' Ruth said, when they were in the ladies. 'I hope she doesn't have to go to an unmarried mother's home. The nuns treat you like a slut. If only she'd got him to use a condom.'

Jo shrugged. 'She's Catholic. Maybe she doesn't believe in birth control. Maybe it's him.'

Later, when Jo told Ian, he said, 'Poor kid.'

'Maybe I should go on the pill,' Jo said.

Ian shook his head. 'You know I'm careful.'

'What if it breaks?'

'What if you forget to take the pill?'

She stared at him. Didn't he trust her? 'I wouldn't.'

Ian shrugged. 'If the worst happens, we'll work something out.'

Was she supposed to get an abortion, creeping into some strange woman's house like a thief? Or would he reluctantly offer to marry her, like he had Ange? Jo didn't ask. She didn't want to know the answer.

...

Over the next couple of weeks, a tense feeling hung in the office as Jenny waited for Jimmy to come back from Hamburg. Susie and Christina fussed over Jenny like mother hens, and Jo and Ruth took turns to fetch a sandwich for her from downstairs, cheese and chutney in white bread. Halfway through the third week, Jenny came into work, her face lit up. She and Jimmy were getting married. They'd been up to Ballarat to ask her father's permission and he'd said yes. She was having a tiny wedding. Only her family, her landlady and the landlady's son were coming. She was going to wear a pink dress and her sister, who worked in a flower shop, would make her bouquet.

Presents started arriving on Jenny's desk: a set of six teaspoons in a navy box patterned with gold stars, a pair of yellow pottery salt and pepper shakers from the gift shop downstairs, four blue and white checked tea towels (an unpleasant reminder of Maureen's approaching kitchen tea), a wooden salad bowl and a basket with a fabric liner for scones.

Jenny went to the hairdressers and came back with her brown hair streaked blonde. Her breasts and hips were more rounded, her belly swelling.

Christina said that Jenny would be a beautiful woman when she got older. 'See those curves,' she said. 'And she has the pretty face.' She shot Jo a sideways glance. 'You should eat more.'

Jo realised with a horrible sinking feeling that she was jealous of Jenny. Everyone was glad that Jenny was getting married, but if Jo told them she was living with Ian, there'd be no congratulations or presents, just shocked looks and gossip. One lunchtime she went downstairs to the gift shop and bought a pair of geometric patterned mugs, which she asked to have gift wrapped. When she got upstairs, she put them in the bottom of her basket to take home.

Later, at Ian's flat, when she unwrapped them he said, 'Why did you buy those? We don't need them.'

She pouted. 'I liked them.' She didn't tell him it was because of Jenny.

Sitting at the table, she ripped open her pay packet. Pushing a couple of bank notes towards him, she said, 'This is for my share of the food.'

Ian shook his head. 'I don't want it.'

'Don't be so old-fashioned,' she said.

He glared at her. 'So, I'm old-fashioned, am I, having my eighteen-year-old girlfriend living with me?'

Her bottom lip trembled. 'I want to help,' she said in a low voice.

'I know, but don't talk about money.'

She lit a cigarette.

'I wish you'd cut down,' Ian said. 'They're bad for your health. Haven't you seen the ads?'

She had. Large billboards on railway stations displaying a picture of a newspaper article with the headline Lung Cancer Deaths Up and a tin ashtray of cigarette butts, their ends stained with red lipstick. Disgusting.

'I can't give up yet,' she said.

'I didn't ask you to give up. I said to try and cut down.'

How could she cut down when she felt so stressed?

'Not yet,' she said.

…

Ian got up and went into the living room. He sat on the couch, picked up his copy of *The Herald*, and dropped it on the floor. He looked up as Jo appeared in the doorway.

'I'm sorry,' she said. 'I didn't mean to make you mad.'

'Do you know how I feel when you offer me money?' he asked.

'No.'

'That I'm too tight to pay for you.' He'd leave out the humiliation of knowing he couldn't afford it.

She was leaning against the door jamb. As usual he was struck by her beauty. 'If I was sharing the flat and I wasn't your girlfriend you wouldn't care.'

'That's true, but you are.'

'Please. Let me give you what I used to pay Betty.'

Ian sighed. It went against the grain, but he knew he was too broke to refuse. It would serve the miserable old cow right that he was getting it instead of her. 'Alright,' he said, 'but I don't like it.'

...

Maureen called. 'I'm gonna have a nervous breakdown,' she said. 'Dad's shot through.'

Jo's breath caught in her throat. 'Has he got another woman?'

'Don't be ridiculous,' Maureen said. 'Dad's too old for that.'

'Why, then?'

'Why?' Maureen echoed in mock surprise. 'Because of you living with Ian, of course. Dad must have had enough of Mum going on about it.'

Maureen's words burned into Jo's brain. It was her fault.

'Do you know where he is?'

'The Springvale Caravan Park,' Maureen said. 'Michael and me went to see him last night.'

'Is he alright?'

'He seemed alright, but Mum's on another planet,' Maureen said. 'She says if anyone asks where Dad is, we're to say he's on a fishing trip. It's pathetic, but Mum hates being shown up. Even Father Brady doesn't know. The only person who does is Robbie. She's over here a lot.'

If Jo hadn't left home this would never have happened.

'I reckon if you go and talk to Dad, you might persuade him to come home,' Maureen said. 'You've always been his favourite. He asked about you last night.'

Jo's grip on the phone tightened. 'What did you say?'

'That you were fine. Michael and me can pick you up if Ian doesn't want to take you.'

One of Maureen's sneaky moves to find out where Jo and Ian were living. 'No, it'll be fine,' Jo said.

'Can you go and see him tonight? The wedding's only four weeks away.'

The bloody wedding.

'I'll call you tomorrow,' Maureen said. 'Bye.'

Jo put down the receiver and went into Ian's cubicle. 'What's wrong?' he asked.

'That was Maureen. Dad's left Mum. He's living at the Springvale Caravan Park. She wants me to go see him tonight.'

Ian raised his eyebrows. 'Wants?'

Jo felt a flicker of irritation. 'She asked me to try and talk him into going home. The wedding's in four weeks.'

Ian scowled. 'So, it's all about getting him home so she can have the perfect wedding. There's no consideration for what *he* wants.'

Jo's eyes opened wider. Why hadn't she thought of that herself? 'Will you take me?' she asked.

'Will you listen to him instead of doing what your sister wants?'

Jo nodded. 'Yes.'

'Alright.'

'Thanks.' Jo went back to her desk and sat down. She'd always known that Maureen was bossy, but she was only just starting to see how unthinkingly she did what Maureen wanted.

...

Ian watched Jo go back to her desk. She was obviously in shock. He was surprised Kev had had the guts to leave. That wife of his was a religious nutcase. He'd take Jo to see Kev tonight, but he had no intention of getting involved. Already his guts churned with old feelings of helplessness and rage.

...

That night, Jo knocked on the door of Kev's caravan. Light glowed around the curtains that had been pulled across the windows. The door opened, and Kev stood in the entrance wearing a pair of trousers and one of his old cardigans. She felt a rush of tenderness.

His expression changed to surprise. 'Hello, love, come in.'

She stepped inside, and they hugged.

'Have a seat,' he said. 'Would you like a beer?'

'Thanks.' Jo sat on a bench next to the small table and looked around. Everything in the caravan was neat, from the washing up in a rack beside the tiny sink, to the cover without a wrinkle on the double bed at the far end. The air smelt of fish and chips and the sharp tang of pickled onion.

Kev got a bottle of beer out of the tiny fridge. He flipped off the cap, poured the beer into glasses, brought them over to the table.

Jo picked up her glass.

'Cheers,' Kev said.

'Cheers.' Jo swallowed some beer. 'How are you?'

Kev made a wry face. 'Enjoying the peace.'

'I've been worried about you.'

'You think I've gone nuts?'

'No, I didn't mean that. It was so unexpected.'

Kev looked at his hands resting on the table. 'To be honest, I've been thinking about it for years.'

Jo couldn't hide her surprise.

'I haven't made your mother happy. She wanted me to have my own business, but I'm fine working for someone else. The still births didn't help.'

He'd never spoken their names. Patrick, born two years after Kathleen, Frances a year later.

Kev swallowed some beer. 'She got more religious after that. Before we were married, she was different.' He put down his glass and pulled a packet of cigarettes out of the pocket of his cardigan. 'Want one?'

'Thanks.'

Kev struck a match and lit their cigarettes. Blowing out smoke, he asked, 'How are things with you?'

'Good,' she said. What else could she say when he'd left Mum and lived in a caravan?

'I don't like that you're living together,' Kev said. 'You should get married.'

Jo stared at him in surprise. 'Don't you care about church doctrine?'

Kev shook his head. 'No, love. I reckon God's got a lot more kindness than what the church says.'

Jo reached out and touched the back of his hand. 'I love him, Dad.'

'He's a lucky man.'

'What are you going to do?' she asked.

Kev shrugged. 'I'm not sure, but you can tell your sister I'll be giving her away at the wedding. Couldn't tell her last night. She was too busy trying to persuade me to go home. She's a bit like your mother. Got a one-track mind.'

'I wouldn't tell you what to do,' Jo said.

'No, you wouldn't, love,' Kev said. 'Where's Ian?'

'He's waiting outside.'

'Ask him to come in. It's time I got to know him better.'

Maureen's kitchen tea was being held at Michael's parents' house in Mentone. As Jo walked up the path to the verandah her stomach churned. Maureen would have told everyone here that she lived with Ian.

The door opened as she stepped onto the verandah, and Maureen stood in the doorway. 'Come in,' she said. 'We've been waiting for you.'

'Sorry,' Jo said. 'I missed the train.'

Maureen raised her eyebrows. 'I'd have thought Ian would have driven you here.'

Jo wiped her boots on the mat. 'He's gone to karate.'

'I didn't know he did karate.'

'He's just started,' Jo said.

'Mum's not here,' Maureen said. 'She had to do stocktaking.'

Jo felt a surge of relief.

Inside, a patterned carpet, and a musty smell. An old-fashioned pendant light dangled from the ceiling. The living room was through a pair of glass doors. As Jo walked in, she saw a circle of women and girls sitting on dining chairs. There was Renee, who worked with Maureen in the salon, heavily pregnant; a pale, spotty young girl of about sixteen; Michael's mother Frances, a thin little woman with a nervous laugh;

another larger woman about the same age; and Maureen's friends Christine and Jackie. Jackie's child, a boy of about two, sat on the floor at her feet eating potato chips out of a packet and dropping crumbs on the carpet.

'Here's my other bridesmaid,' Maureen announced. 'My sister, Jo.'

Everyone stared at Jo.

'This is Jean,' Maureen said, waving an arm towards the older woman, then the pale spotty girl. 'Lizzie, my apprentice.'

Jean didn't smile. Lizzie did.

'Nice to meet you,' Jo said.

Frances had jumped up from her chair. 'Would you like some punch?' she asked. 'It's non-alcoholic.'

Jo wished it was. 'Yes, please.' She sat in the empty chair next to Kathleen. The briquette heater in the fireplace glowed red and she was starting to sweat.

Frances returned with a glass of punch.

Jo took a sip. It was cold and fizzy and tasted of lemon and pineapple juice.

'Now that Jo's here, we can play a game,' Maureen said.

Jo gulped the punch down. Why hadn't she twigged they'd be playing stupid party games?

Maureen whipped off a checked tea towel that covered a breakfast tray. The tray was set with different items including a spoon, a clock and a pencil sharpener. 'There's twelve things,' Maureen said. 'Have a good look before I cover it up.'

But Jo was looking at Jackie. She and her husband and little boy had just moved into a new house on the housing estate behind Jo's parents' house. When Jo's family moved into their house three years ago, an old blue farmhouse stood across the paddock, and a herd of black and white cows used to graze over the back fence. Now the old blue farmhouse and the cows were gone, the paddock crisscrossed by roads and newly built houses. Those houses would fill up with people like Jacky and her husband and their little boy, and newlyweds, like Maureen and Michael. They'd have babies and watch them grow up. There'd be birthday parties and neighbourhood barbeques, and the women would all get on because they had everything they wanted, marriage and kids and a house, while Jo would have no wedding ring on her finger, no baby and no new house. She and Ian were poor, he was paying for Anna until she left school. But if Jo was being honest, she wasn't sure if she wanted that kind of life. She remembered Helen, and Ingrid, who weren't particularly happy. If only people, including her mother, were kinder about people living together, she might feel better.

They played the memory game, which Kathleen won, and then another.

Halfway through the game, the family dog, an old black labrador with a grizzled muzzle, brought in a blackbird and dropped it at Frances's feet. Frances screamed and shot out of her chair, while Kathleen darted over and picked up the bird.

'Dead,' she said.

Frances went to get an old newspaper, and Kathleen wrapped the blackbird in newspaper sheets and took it outside.

Some people, including Jean, left the room and Frances went around offering more punch. Jo got up to go to the toilet, but it was occupied. A minute or so later, the door of the toilet opened, and Jean came out. She looked Jo up and down, eyes slitted. 'You little slut,' she said. 'You should be ashamed of yourself.'

Jo went into the toilet and collapsed onto the seat. She cried until her throat ached, took out a hankie and wiped her tears away. Looking down she saw that her skirt was halfway up her thighs. Ian said she was sexy. Jean was probably jealous. She was a nasty old cow with a fat bum.

Someone turned the handle of the locked toilet door. Jo took a deep breath. She got up, flushed the toilet, and opened the door. Renee stood outside, 'Sorry, she said. 'The baby's dropped. I can't stop peeing.'

When everyone was back in the living room, Maureen opened her presents, which were as boring as Jo expected, including hers, a pair of wooden salad servers. As the afternoon wore on, she felt as if she was looking at people through a thick plate of glass. She listened to Lizzie talking about her boyfriend and Jacky about having another baby while Kathleen kept giving her concerned looks. By the end of the afternoon, Jo felt dead inside. Walking towards the station she marvelled at how a few horrible words from someone she didn't know could have turned her into such a mess.

On the train she curled up in the corner of a nearly empty carriage and cried silently. She'd thought she could handle people being judgemental, but she couldn't. She was pathetic.

...

Ian looked up from *Farewell My Lovely* as Jo walked in. She looked like she'd been crying for hours. Why the hell had she gone to the bloody kitchen tea, anyway?

'Hello, sweetheart,' he said. He went over and put his arms around her. 'I thought we'd go out for tea.'

'Alright.'

Her voice sounded flat, uninterested. 'What's the matter?' he asked.

'Jean upset me.'

He felt a flicker of impatience. 'Who's Jean?'

'A woman I met today. She called me a slut and said I should be ashamed of myself.' Tears spilled down Jo's cheeks. 'She looked at me like I was something that had crawled out of a drain.'

It wasn't his idea that they live together.

She must have thought the same because her face changed. 'I'm sorry, I didn't mean—

'If you're getting this upset, maybe you should think about living somewhere else,' he said.

She ran into the bedroom.

Seconds later, he heard loud sobbing. *Jesus.* Going into the bedroom he saw her lying face down on the bed. He went over and sat down next to her. 'I don't understand how a woman you don't know says something nasty and you're broken-hearted. What happens if they find out at work?'

Jo pulled out her hankie and mopped her face. 'It'd be different. They know us.'

'Nice people can have strong ideas about what's right and wrong, especially sex and marriage,' he said.

Jo folded her hanky into a tiny square. 'I'd be prepared for that. I'm upset because Jean was judging me, and she doesn't know either of us.'

'People do it all the time,' he said.

'I hate it.'

'It's life.'

She rolled over and looked up at him. 'Do you really want me to leave?'

'I didn't say that.' Ian ran a hand around his jaw. 'It's all happened too fast.'

She looked appalled. 'But you said you wanted to make me happy.'

'Are you?'

She shook her head. 'It's my fault my family split up.'

'Your family was in the shit a long time before you moved in with me,' he said. 'You've nothing to feel guilty about.'

'But I do.'

He sighed. 'Look, I've had enough family dramas of my own. I don't want yours as well.'

'I'm sorry,' Jo said. 'I won't mention them.'

Ian frowned. 'That's useless. You need to separate from them.'

Her eyes widened. 'You mean not see them?'

'No, just remember that you don't have to get caught up in their dramas.'

Her shoulders drooped. 'You're judging my family.'

'I'm sorry you feel like that,' he said. 'I'm trying to help.'

She stood up and put on her coat.

'Where are you going?' he asked.

'Out.'

'Don't be too long. I've booked a restaurant.'

She didn't answer.

Ian watched her walk out. He didn't know how to handle her when she was like this. It made him feel angry and frustrated. If she didn't come back soon he'd go to the restaurant by himself. He went over to the window, saw her disappear up the street.

...

Outside, lights shone from the windows of the surrounding flats, and there were no stars. A cold wind blew in from Port Phillip Bay. Jo shivered. It was madness to be out here by herself. She imagined Jean sitting on the old-fashioned dining chair across from her in Frances's living room and blew a stream of smoke in her direction. *Up yours, fat-arsed cow.*

Tears filled her eyes. *He doesn't love me enough.*

A couple came towards her, holding hands. They looked about the same age as Jo. The boy said something to the girl, and she laughed. Jo felt a ripple of envy as they walked past. Maybe they were going home to make love. She and Ian had been like that until she'd moved in with him. She'd given him no choice, just turned up one Sunday night with her things heaped outside his door. Howling over Jean was the worst thing she could do. She had to stop showing how devastated she felt. Dropping her cigarette butt on the pavement, she stamped on it with her foot and turned to go home.

When she entered Ian's flat, he was sitting on the couch holding a glass of beer. He looked up at her with a wary expression.

'I'm sorry,' she said. 'I overreacted.'

She walked over and knelt beside him. 'Don't be mad at me. Let's go out and have fun.'

He swallowed some beer. 'It's been a while since we've done that.'

She felt as if she'd been slapped, but she wouldn't show it. 'Well, it's time we did it again.' She took his glass of beer and swallowed some. She gave it back.

Ian finished his beer and went out to the kitchen. He still felt annoyed, but he'd get over it. Ange had never said she was sorry about anything.

…

Maureen rang on Monday. 'What was the matter with you on Saturday?' she asked. 'You were like a zombie.'

'I had a headache,' Jo said.

'I'm calling about Mum.'

Oh God.

'She's depressed,' Maureen said. 'It's a shame you couldn't talk Dad into coming home.'

'He doesn't want to.'

'This is what it's like at home,' Maureen said. 'Mum goes to early morning mass, comes home, dunks a biscuit into a cup of tea and goes to work. She's working full time now because she's paying the bills. When she gets home, she's too tired to cook, so Kathleen's taken over.'

'Horrible,' Jo said.

'Exactly,' Maureen said. 'It's a wonder we haven't all had food poisoning. We need someone to come and help.'

'What about Auntie Eileen?'

'She and Mum fight.'

'Yes, but they're sisters. If anyone can make Mum laugh it's her.'

'Alright, I'll call her,' Maureen said, and hung up.

Half an hour later, she called back. 'Auntie Eileen's coming for ten days. She can't stay any longer 'cause she's going on a car rally.'

It must be Auntie Eileen's latest thing. She'd gone through quite a few of them over the years, ranging from gemstone hunting to learning how to play bridge.

'Fab,' Jo breathed. If anyone could get Mum out of her depression it would be Auntie Eileen.

...

Ian watched Jo as she talked on the phone. The caller would be Maureen the drama queen, giving Jo the day's update. If Maureen was his sister, he'd tell her to get lost. When Jo came back from her walk on Saturday, she'd been almost back to normal. They'd gone to a new Japanese restaurant and eaten raw fish. Afterwards, they drank sake. Under its influence, Jo had told him that she liked him going to karate because she could read while he was away. Then she started talking about how she loved exploring rock pools, and how she'd spent hours as a child lying on her stomach watching tiny fish darting through the water, crabs scuttling about on the bottom, and sea anemones that looked like flowers but were in fact animals.

She said when she was younger she'd dreamed of sailing around the world in a small boat, but realised how stupid it was because whenever she was on a boat she got sick. He'd poured her more sake because he liked her being like this, relaxed and happy. She'd said she didn't talk about books much because her mother said men didn't like clever girls, but she thought it was wrong, and he said she could be as clever as she liked so long as she understood she wasn't cleverer than him. This sent her into fits of laugher. He said she'd find out how clever he was by teaching her how to play chess, but she said she hated board games.

She'd leaned towards him, a serious look on her face. 'I want you to teach me how to live,' she said, as if he had some magic formula. If she found out he didn't have a clue, she'd be appalled.

She'd bought lavender and geraniums for the balcony. To his surprise, they were thriving. She'd scavenged the beach for shells and bits of sea glass to put in their pots and made sure they were watered. Looking after plants made her feel relaxed, she said, but she was smoking too much, and the red rash on her wrist was still there. At night she sneaked out onto the balcony to have a last cigarette. He suspected she was unhappy most of the time.

Chapter Twenty-three

Along Swanston Street the trees were opening soft green leaves, but Jo's stomach fluttered as she got off the tram with Ian. Today she was going to tell her workmates she was living with him. When she'd mentioned it to him yesterday, he'd said, 'If you want.' She'd been shocked.

'Don't you care?' she asked.

He shrugged. 'Doesn't matter if you've decided.'

'But what do you think?'

'It's a bad idea.'

'I'm sorry,' she said. 'I have to be honest.'

They walked up Collins Street past the old stone churches and the small window of Le Louvre that displayed a leather handbag and silk scarf that would cost about a year of Jo's pay. She wouldn't want them anyway.

When they entered Coates Building, Ian said, 'Good luck,' and disappeared up the stairs.

Jo's heart thumped. After today, he wouldn't have to do it anymore.

In the girls' room, Christina sat on the couch sewing a button onto her cardigan. Jo's plan to tell the first person she saw vanished. Christina looked up, said, 'How are you?'

'Fine,' Jo said as she hung up her coat. 'You?'

Christina cut the thread with a pair of nail scissors and slipped them into her make-up bag. 'Good. How was your weekend?'

'I went to my sister's kitchen tea.'

You little slut. Jo bit her lip. Why couldn't she forget that old bag?

Christina snapped her handbag shut. 'What is a kitchen tea, please?'

'It's like a party when someone's getting married. You bring presents for their kitchen, like tea towels and wooden spoons.'

Christina's expression turned to disgust. 'That is not a party. Parties are for dancing, and eating and drinking.'

Jo's forehead itched. She lifted her hair and stared at the fine red rash on her skin. 'I had to go. I'm my sister's bridesmaid.'

'And you want to marry Ian,' Christina said. 'But he likes to be free.'

Susie clattered in, pert and bright-eyed, followed by Jenny, rounded in the belly, a gold wedding ring on her finger. Jo said hello and went out to the office. Yes, she wanted to marry Ian, but she didn't want a marriage like her mother, or Ingrid, or Helen. And if there came a perfect day when Ian asked her to marry him, it still wouldn't fix things with her mother, because he was divorced. Plus, he didn't want more kids, and Jo couldn't bear it if she had none, even though she didn't like kids much. She reached for a cigarette and lit up. She'd do anything for Ian, but he wouldn't for her. Why hadn't she fallen in love with someone who wanted the same things she did?

As the morning wore on, Jo smoked cigarette after cigarette, wondering if she was brave enough to tell anyone about her and Ian. At last, she spotted Moira leaving the office. Moira lived with Ollie. She would understand. Jo went into the corridor, and spotted Moira disappearing into the ladies' toilets. Jo hurried down the corridor and pushed open the door. In the mirror her face looked white.

Moira emerged from a stall. Around her neck hung a string of small pearls.

'Nice pearls,' Jo said, although she wouldn't be seen dead in them herself.

'Thank you,' Moira said. 'They were a present from Ollie.' She went over to the taps and turned them on.

'How long have you been living with him?' Jo asked.

Moira's jaw dropped.

'I'm sorry,' Jo said, 'I was being nosy.'

'I don't share my personal life, Jo.'

Jo's face burned. 'I'm living with Ian.'

In the mirror she saw Moira's calm expression turn to shock.

'We love each other,' Jo added.

Moira turned off the taps. 'I'm sure you do, but you have no idea what you've got yourself into. When a couple live together the man gets away with it, but the woman is called unpleasant names.'

You little slut.

'I know,' Jo said. 'It's happened already.'

'And you're not protected by the law,' Moira said. 'If you and Ian live together and split up, you'll get nothing.

Jo wrinkled her nose. 'He doesn't own much.'

Moira nodded. 'I suppose his wife got everything. But if you and Ian saved up to buy a flat, and you split up, it would be in his name – *even if you helped to pay for it.*'

Jo hadn't expected Moira to talk about money and the law. All she cared about was love.

'Ollie and I want our own place, but I won't buy anything until we're married,' Moira said. 'If the law was different, I probably wouldn't.' She touched Jo's arm. 'You're looking very stressed, dear.'

Jo's eyes filled with tears. 'My parents split up.'

'Oh, I'm sorry,' Moira said. 'That's a lot to cope with. Come and talk to me whenever you like. But please, don't mention anything to the others about living together. You've got enough on your plate.'

'No-one talks about you and Ollie,' Jo said.

Moira gave a tiny smile. 'We're old, and we've both had broken marriages. You've got your whole life ahead of you. It would be a shame to ruin it.'

'I came in this morning determined to tell people,' Jo said. 'And the first person I met was Christina, so I didn't say anything.'

Moira nodded. 'Sensible girl. I'm sorry to tell you this, but you won't find anyone who thinks it's a good idea, not even Christina.'

It hit Jo like a thunderclap that what she really wanted was for some-one to congratulate her and wish her and Ian happiness, but it seemed that was only for people who were getting married. 'Alright, I'll keep it to myself,' she said.

Moira nodded. 'It's for the best,' she said. 'Who knows? You might end up getting married to Ian, and everyone will be happy for you.'

At lunchtime, when they were eating their sandwiches, Jo told Ian that after talking with Moira she'd changed her mind.

He grinned. 'Good old Moira. It's nice to know I don't have to pick up the pieces.'

Jo felt a ripple of resentment. She was stronger than he thought.

...

Ian flexed his sore shoulders. He'd gone to karate last night. His part-ner was Doug, a little older, tough and decent. Ian suspected that Doug might have had a few problems growing up. It was in his watchfulness, and the pale scar along his jaw that could have been made by a knife. There was a mutual respect between them, the sense they might have had a similar past.

...

Maureen called Jo. 'Auntie Eileen's here. She's sleeping in your bed, and she snores. I hate it.'

'How's she getting on with Mum?' Jo asked.

'They had a couple of fights, but they're alright now,' Maureen said. 'And guess what? Auntie Eileen went round to see Dad and he's coming here next Wednesday night to talk about the wedding. Auntie Eileen thinks Ian should come. She and Mum had a big fight about it. Mum said no, but I want you to ask him again.'

'He'll say no,' Jo said.

'Can you please ask?'

'I told you he doesn't like weddings.'

'He'll come if you want him to, won't he?'

'No.'

'It sounds to me like he does what he wants, and you go along with it.'

The rash on Jo's wrist itched. 'It's not like that. He wants to make me happy.'

'Well, tell him he'll make you happy if he comes.'

'I'll let you know.'

'Tomorrow, please.'

Maureen hung up. Jo lit a cigarette. She'd ask Ian, but she already knew the answer.

...

'No,' Ian said.

Jo made a face. 'Please. I want us to dance at the reception.'

'You don't like ballroom dancing.'

'We can jive, can't we?'

'If you want to dance with me, we can go to a ball.'

She pouted. 'Why won't you go?'

'I don't believe in weddings.'

'But I want you to see me all dressed up.'

He reached under the table and put his hand under her skirt. 'I prefer you undressed.' She wriggled closer. 'I think you do, too,' he said.

Later, in bed, she said to him, 'So you won't go.'

He turned and looked at her in the half dark. At night her hair looked almost black, her blue eyes dark. 'No,' he said. 'I won't change my mind.'

...

At lunchtime the next day, Maureen called. 'What did he say?'

'No,' Jo said.

Silence, then Maureen said, 'I'm so disappointed. I wanted him there.'

'I don't know why,' Jo said. 'It's not like he's family or anything.'

'But you're living with him, so he is.'

'I told you before. He doesn't believe in marriage.'

'If he really loved you, he'd want to marry you,' Maureen said. 'And he'd want to have kids with you.'

Jo slammed down the phone and stormed towards the door.

In the toilets she pressed her hot face against the cool wall. She heard the door to the toilets open and Ruth's voice said, 'Jo, are you alright?'

'I'm so bloody angry.'

'Golly,' Ruth said, 'You sound it. Come out.'

Jo opened the door. Ruth stood outside in her green miniskirt and white lace pantyhose, her auburn hair cut in the latest style, a bob, shingled at the back.

'Maureen's such a cow,' Jo said, going over to the taps.

'What did she do?' Ruth asked.

Jo turned on the cold tap, splashed water onto her face. 'She said if Ian really loved me he'd marry me and give me kids.' She turned off the tap. 'I'm so jealous of Ange. She was married to him and had Anna and she didn't appreciate it.'

'Stop thinking about her,' Ruth said. 'You're the one living with him.'

Jo stared at her miserable face in the mirror. Why couldn't she be satisfied with what she had?

'You'll probably marry him anyway,' Ruth said. 'Come on. Let's go back, or Moira will come to check on us.'

When they got back to the office, Christina had left a cup of her disgusting chamomile tea on Jo's desk. Jo looked across at her, mouthed *thank you.*

As Jo raised the cup to her lips, the door of the office opened, and Ian walked in. He looked across at her and smiled. She forced herself to smile back.

Chapter Twenty-four

The following Saturday Jo got off the tram and walked along St Kilda Road. Splashes of sunlight lay on the pavement, filtering through the new leaves of the trees. Her footsteps slowed as she approached her Auntie Eileen's block of flats, which were almost hidden by large trees. Jo walked past the side garden, filled with evergreen shrubs that stank of tom cats, and climbed the metal staircase to the second floor.

Auntie Eileen's front door was painted a dull green, with an oval window of thick glass. Jo stood for a minute or two before she knocked.

The door opened to a smell of baking and Auntie Eileen, red-cheeked, stood in the entrance, a blue and white checked tea towel over one shoulder. 'Come in,' she said. 'Give me a hug.'

Hugging Auntie Eileen was like hugging a jellyfish, or what Jo imagined hugging a jellyfish would feel like. She was soft, and you couldn't feel her bones. When they drew apart, Auntie Eileen said, 'You've come at exactly the right time. I've just got the scones out of the oven.'

Jo followed her auntie into the dim living room, which was full of old-fashioned furniture.

'Sit down, dear. I'll bring in the scones.' Auntie Eileen disappeared into the tiny kitchen as Jo plonked herself down on the couch. Glancing around, she saw that everything still looked the same. The carved Victorian sideboard stood against the wall, the pair of china dalmatians stared at her from their places on the mantelpiece and the sunburst clock hung on the wall above. Jo had always thought these things were hideous, but today they seemed comforting. It was easy to imagine that life went on here year after year without any nasty surprises.

Auntie Eileen emerged from the kitchen with a dark blue wooden tray on which stood an old-fashioned plate piled with scones, and bowls of jam and whipped cream. She put the tray on the coffee table. 'I'll be back with the tea.'

While she was in the kitchen, Jo stuck a finger into the bowl of whipped cream and licked it.

Auntie Eileen came back with a tray of tea things and set it on the coffee table.

'Well,' she said, sinking into the well-padded armchair opposite. 'I see you haven't been able to resist the cream. I used to drink bottles of it when I was young.'

Jo smiled. It was the kind of thing Auntie Eileen would do.

'Have a scone,' Auntie Eileen urged.

Jo helped herself to a knife and plate, and cut into a scone, spreading it thickly with jam and cream.

'I'm so glad to be home,' Auntie Eileen said. 'It's been a difficult ten days.'

Jo took a bite of her scone.

'Your mother's mortified that Kev's left, and she's worried about you.'

'I'm fine,' Jo said.

Auntie Eileen handed Jo a cup of tea. 'Of course, you are, dear. You're a brave girl. But I didn't invite you here to talk about your parents. I thought I'd lend you some moral support. If I told you something about my life, you'd realise that you can live quite happily without getting married.'

Jo's eyes widened.

'I had a lover for many years,' Auntie Eileen continued. 'Duncan died when I was fifty-three.' Auntie Eileen's voice softened. 'He was ten years older than me, and married, with three boys. I met him when I was eighteen.'

'What about your fiancé?'

'There never was one,' Auntie Eileen said. 'It was just your mother's way of coping with the fact that I had a lifelong affair with Duncan.'

Jo frowned. 'So, she lied.'

'Your mother finds it hard to look at life as it really is, so she invents things.'

Jo swallowed the last of her scone. For years, Mum had told her that Auntie Eileen was a pathetic old spinster who had no self-control with alcohol. Yet here she was on a Saturday afternoon, stone cold sober, drinking tea and eating scones. And tomorrow she was going on a car rally. Mum was wrong. How many other things had she been wrong about?

'You've fallen in love with an older man who's been married, but unlike me, you live with him,' Auntie Eileen said. 'Good for you.'

Jo felt herself filling up with happiness.

Auntie Eileen leaned forward. 'Your mother used to call me feckless, but I've had more fun than her ten times over.' She smiled. 'So will you if you ignore all the naysayers. But it won't be easy.'

'I know,' Jo said. 'Moira at work was horrified, and this woman at Maureen's kitchen tea called me a slut.'

'Do the others at work know?' Auntie Eileen asked.

Jo shook her head. 'Moira told me not to tell anyone. Ian did too.'

'They're trying to protect you, dear. Have another scone.'

'You're the first person who approves of us,' Jo said. 'Even Dad said he wished we could get married.'

'He's trying to protect you as well.'

'Why do people have to be so nasty?'

Auntie Eileen sipped her tea. 'Because you're doing something different. It unsettles people, particularly the ones who are unhappily married. They see you, a young girl with a handsome lover, and compare their lives to yours. And they get angry.'

Jo's voice trembled. 'But what if it doesn't last?'

'No-one knows how long their love affairs will last, dear. You might be lucky and have it last as long as mine.'

Jo helped herself to another scone. 'Do you regret not getting married or having kids?'

'When I fell in love with Duncan, I made my choice,' Auntie Eileen said. 'You can't have everything you want. Duncan's children were still quite young when his wife was diagnosed with MS. He felt he had to stay. I loved him for himself, not for what he could give me.'

'I think you're a saint,' Jo said.

Auntie Eileen picked up another scone. 'Not at all. I loved him.'

'That's how I feel about Ian,' Jo said. 'I wish I could stop believing that I can't be totally happy unless we get married and have kids.' Was it something that all girls felt, or because she'd been told for years that her destiny was marriage and motherhood?

Auntie Eileen's face softened. 'You're only eighteen, dear. Why worry about something you have no control over?'

'I reckon I'd die if we split.'

Auntie Eileen shook her head. 'You'd grieve, then you'd pick yourself up and get on with life.'

'It would feel so empty.'

'Life is exciting, dear.'

Jo stared at her. Auntie Eileen was three years older than Mum, but there was still something young about her.

'You're probably feeling more vulnerable right now because your mum and dad have separated,' Auntie Eileen said. 'It even surprised me.'

'I wish they'd get back together.'

Auntie Eileen raised an eyebrow. 'Why? Do you think your dad was happy before he left?'

'No,' Jo said. 'He spent most of his time in the shed.'

'Because he couldn't stand being in the house with your mother.'

It was probably true.

'I didn't want to come today,' Jo said. 'I thought you'd go on at me about Mum.'

'No,' Auntie Eileen said. 'I wanted to make sure you were alright. You've made a big decision and your family didn't help.'

Jo's hands twisted together. 'Tell me more about you.'

Auntie Eileen put down her cup. 'I got expelled from school when I was fifteen for smoking in the toilets, so I got a job at Coles Cafeteria in the city. I wanted to be a secretary, so I went to night school twice a week to learn shorthand and typing. After classes, this other girl and I used to go to a milk bar in Elizabeth Street. We always had the same treat, three scoops of vanilla ice cream with chocolate sauce and crushed nuts in a cut glass dish.' Auntie Eileen smiled. 'It's funny how you remember the little things. When I finished my course I got a job as a typist, and when I was eighteen, became a secretary to Duncan. Our affair started soon after. I moved out of home, and Duncan helped me rent a flat. He used to visit me as often as he could. Your mother was horrified. She said I was throwing my life away, and her all of fifteen.'

Jo pulled a face. 'She said the same thing to me.'

Auntie Eileen made the barking sound that was her version of a laugh. 'That's because you're not doing what she thinks is right. You and Kathleen will both be happier than Maureen. That girl is heading for disaster. Imagine her disappointment when she finds out she's expected to live happily ever after in her new house, vacuuming and washing dishes with a bucket of dirty nappies waiting in the laundry.'

'She was having doubts about getting married,' Jo said. 'One night she flirted with Ian. I was so angry.'

'As you should be. I'm sure he's a handsome man.'

'Very.' Jo opened her handbag and pulled out a small photo from an inside pocket. It had been taken one Saturday when they'd squeezed into the tiny photo booth at Flinders Street Station. In the photo she was grinning like a Cheshire cat, but he looked like a film star. She handed the photo to Auntie Eileen.

'He looks a bit cheeky to me,' she said. 'As if he's got his hand up your skirt.'

Jo giggled. 'He did.'

Auntie Eileen made the barking sound again. 'And in a couple of weeks, we've got the wedding. Is Ian coming?'

'No,' Jo said. 'He hates weddings.'

'Because his marriage was awful.'

'Yes.'

'Do you like his daughter?'

Jo shifted on the couch. 'She's nice, but it's hard looking after kids. She had a nightmare after we went to the zoo, and I thought we'd had a good time.'

'I remember feeling very jealous of Duncan's children. He adored them.'

Jo stared at her. Was she jealous of Anna? Yes, a little. She'd felt a nasty little tug of it watching Anna clinging to him, how he'd pulled her closer, smoothing her hair. Did Ian love his daughter more than her? Probably. Telling herself it was a different kind of love didn't help.

'Sometimes I feel it's not fair that Ange had Ian's baby and I won't get the chance,' Jo said. 'He doesn't want more children.'

'Maureen told me,' Auntie Eileen said. 'But who knows what's in store for you both? People do change their minds. Still,' Auntie Eileen continued, 'my best advice to you is to be grateful for what you have and stop worrying about the future. Now dear, I'll just clear these away. I've got friends coming to play bridge at five o'clock.'

Jo's mum said Auntie Eileen was addicted to bridge. 'It's a card game played by old spinsters and widows who've got nothing better to do,' she'd said.

'Do you think Mum can change?' Jo asked, as she got to her feet.

Auntie Eileen shrugged. 'It's up to her.'

They hugged.

'You're too thin, dear,' Auntie Eileen said. 'You need to eat more.'

They drew apart.

'I'll see you at the wedding,' Auntie Eileen said. 'Do try not to step on Maureen's train.'

Jo giggled. 'She says we have to be extra careful if it rains.'

Auntie Eileen opened the front door. 'Maureen will have a perfect day whatever the weather does. Good luck with everything, dear.'

'Thanks,' Jo said, as she stepped out onto the sun dappled balcony. Birds sang among the leaves and from St Kilda Road came the rumble of trams. For a moment she felt as light as air.

Chapter Twenty-five

Ian and Mary sat on a bench at Alphington Park while Anna practised cartwheels on the grass. People walked past with dogs on leads, and a group of teenage boys played football on the oval.

'You haven't said much about Jo today,' Mary said, smiling at Anna as she did a perfect cartwheel. 'Is everything alright?'

'We're fine,' Ian said. 'She's busy.'

'It would be nice to see her again. How about you bring her for tea next Wednesday night?

Ian's belly dropped. 'What time?'

'Half past six,' Mary said. 'I'll cook a roast. Jo likes roasts, doesn't she?'

'Yes.' He watched a teenage boy take a mark on the oval and wished his own life was so carefree. 'Jo's living with me,' he said.

Mary's expression turned to shock. 'Why?'

'She had to leave Ruth's place and she's fallen out with her mother.'

'Because of you.'

Ian shifted a little on the seat. 'Yes.'

'So, what are you going to do about it?' Mary asked.

Ian shrugged. 'Jo's fine.'

'*Jo's fine?*' Mary repeated in an amazed voice. 'If people find out, it could ruin her life. How could you be so selfish?'

Ian scowled. 'She had nowhere to go. What was I supposed to do? Turn her away?'

'No,' Mary said. 'But why did she have to leave her lodgings?'

'Her landlady found out she was spending weekends with me.'

Anna did another perfect cartwheel in front of them. 'Daddy. You're not watching.'

Ian forced himself to smile at her. 'Sorry, sweetie, I'm watching now.'

'If you proposed, wouldn't that put things right with her family?' Mary asked.

'I'm divorced.'

Mary's face changed. 'Oh. Jo's Catholic.'

'Not now.'

'Lapsed,' Mary said in a doleful voice.

Ian frowned. It was another way of saying that once the church got its hooks into you, you'd never be free.

The tinkling of an ice cream van sounded from the street. Anna came running over. 'Daddy, can I have an ice cream?'

Ian stood up and held out his hand. 'Yes, let's go.'

The three of them walked towards the ice cream van. A queue of parents and children had formed in front. They took their places at the back.

Ian looked at Mary. 'Do you want an ice cream?'

Her eyes were cold. 'Yes, please. Strawberry.'

Ian took a couple of steps as the queue moved forward. His mum wanted him to marry Jo, but he didn't like himself when he was married. A memory of the woman he screwed after work one night came into his head. He hadn't even known her name. She'd wanted it as much as he did, but afterwards he felt ashamed. If he married Jo, how did he know he wouldn't do it again? Jo would want a baby, but how could he have another kid when he'd abandoned Anna?

She stood beside him, holding his hand. Her hand was small, the bones fragile. He felt a surge of tenderness.

'Ian.'

He started.

Mary was looking at him with a puzzled expression. 'It's our turn.'

'Right.' He looked at the chalked writing on the blackboard and ordered the ice creams, then reached into his pocket for his wallet, flat and worn, with a few notes inside.

After paying, he and Mary walked across the grass while Anna skipped on ahead.

'How long do you think Jo will stay with you if you don't propose?' Mary asked.

'She loves me,' Ian said. Some vanilla ice cream had run down to his fingers. He licked them clean.

'You should be old enough to realise that love isn't enough,' Mary said.

'It is for me.'

'Sometimes I think you need to grow up a bit more,' Mary said.

...

Jo emerged from the bedroom wearing a navy dress and a pink cardigan. 'Do I look alright?' she asked.

'As long as you've got knickers underneath,' Ian said, smiling when she laughed. 'Honestly, Jo, Mum doesn't care what you wear. She likes you.'

'Have you told her we're living together?'

'She's fine with it.'

'But she's Catholic.'

'She wants me to be happy,' Ian said.

Jo felt a pang. *If only my mum was like that.*

It was dusk when Ian pulled up outside his mum's house. Magpies chortled from the gum trees over the road.

Mary opened the front door as they stepped onto the verandah. 'Come in,' she said.

They stepped inside to the smell of roast lamb.

Mary kissed Jo. It's lovely to see you again.'

'And you,' Jo said.

In the kitchen, the table was set for three with cutlery and paper napkins folded into triangles.

'Is there any beer?' Ian asked, going to the fridge.

'Yes,' Mary said. 'I'll have one too.'

While Ian poured the beer, and opened the wine he'd brought for Jo, Mary bent down to the oven. She pulled out the roasting dish and put it on a wooden board, then lifted the lamb onto a meat tray and covered it with a tea towel.

'Do you want me to make the gravy?' Ian asked.

Mary nodded. 'Yes please.'

Jo sipped on her wine as she watched Ian put the pan on the stove, mixing the leftover juices with flour and water. Mary drained a saucepan of peas in the sink. 'It's just like old times,' she said. 'Me cooking a roast and Ian making the gravy.' She lifted the plates from their rack over the stove and put them at the end of the table. 'Ian says you've been busy.'

'My sister's getting married in two weeks,' Jo said. 'I'm one of the bridesmaids.'

'How lovely,' Mary said.

Ian lifted the pan and poured the gravy into a jug. 'It's a big expensive wedding where people will say nice things and not mean them and eat and drink too much.'

'Most people enjoy a wedding,' Mary said.

'They'd probably enjoy a funeral just as much,' Ian said. 'As long as there's plenty of booze.'

Mary shook her head. 'They're two different things.'

'With a lot of trouble in between.'

To Jo's surprise, Mary laughed. 'There are a few good spots. Like the morning you were born.' She smiled at Ian, her eyes wrinkling at the corners.

Had Jo's mum been pleased when she was born? She'd never said. If Jo ever had a baby, she'd tell that baby every day how much she loved it. And as the baby grew up, there'd be no nagging about the food they didn't eat, or what clothes they wore, and how they had to be polite all the time. The phrase, respect your elders and betters, would never pass her lips.

After Mary dished up the food, they sat around the table.

Mary swallowed some beer. 'I hope you've got a nice suit to wear,' she said to Ian.

'I'm not going,' Ian said.

Mary stared at him. 'Why not?'

'I don't like weddings.'

'That's an awful thing to say. Weddings are lovely.'

'They're fake.'

'Don't be such a naysayer. Not all marriages turn out like yours.'

Ian scowled. 'You can talk.'

'Your father had a bad time in the war. It wasn't all his fault.'

Ian scowled. 'He wrecked our family.'

'Tricia's happily married now, and about to have her second baby,' Mary said. 'I call that a success.'

Jo longed for a cigarette.

'You should go to the wedding for Jo's sake,' Mary said. 'Imagine how she'll feel being on her own.'

'Maureen will have her running round most of the time,' Ian said. 'She won't notice if I'm there or not.'

'I wanted to dance with him at the reception,' Jo said.

Mary looked at Jo. 'Ian's so good at ballroom dancing. He won awards for it when he was a teenager.'

Jo's eyes opened wider. Ian had never mentioned ballroom dancing.

Ian shrugged. 'It was years ago.' He glanced at Jo. 'I told you before, if you want to dance with me, I'll take you to a ball.'

'But I want us to dance at the wedding. It'll be fun.'

Ian shook his head. 'It will not be fun. If I turn up your mother will throw a fit, your sister will get upset, and you'll feel guilty.'

'Maureen wants you to come. She's so disappointed you said no.'

Ian poured more gravy over his food. 'She'll get over it. I'm not changing my mind.'

Mary shook her head. 'That's right, be as stubborn as your father.'

Ian's expression changed. 'I'm not like him.'

'You are in some ways.'

Jo felt a rising panic. 'It's alright. I'll go by myself. Everything will be fine.'

'Of course, it will,' Ian said.

Mary looked at Jo. *He should go with you.*

…

Afterwards, on their way home, Jo sat in a brooding silence.

'What's the matter?' Ian asked.

'You don't love me enough,' she said. 'If you did, you'd come to the wedding.'

He felt a surge of irritation. 'Let's get this straight. If I don't do what you want, I don't love you enough.'

She glared at him. 'You know how petrified I am about going, but you're making me face my family by myself.'

'It's not your family. It's your mother.'

'*And* everyone else. I can't bear to think of them looking at me and thinking I'm a slut.'

'The only person who's called you that is a stranger,' Ian said. 'It's all in your head.'

She stubbed out her cigarette. 'But what if it isn't, and everyone's horrible to me? I'd feel better if I knew you were there.'

'I would be a distraction,' he said. 'Your mother can't stand me.'

Jo slumped against the passenger door and began crying.

Jesus. He pulled over to the side of the road. 'I thought you wanted to be free,' he said. 'But you believe every nasty thing people say to you. The best thing you can do is not go to the wedding.'

Jo got out her hankie, twisting it around a finger. 'I can't do that.'

'You can do anything you like.'

'No, I can't.'

He shrugged. 'I've told you what I think. It's up to you now.'

Jo glared at him. 'I'm going.'

Chapter Twenty-six

On the morning of Maureen's wedding, Jo slid out of bed and went out on the balcony, smelling the lavender and feeling the softness of the geranium leaves. Golden light from the rising sun spilled over blocks of flats, trees and hedges, bouncing off the chrome bumper bars of cars parked in the street. It was going to be a beautiful day.

Below on the pavement, a plump middle-aged woman walked a small black and white dog. Was she married, or did she have a lover? Not a lover. She was too old. But Moira was around the same age, and she had Ollie. Jo lit a cigarette. Inside the flat she heard Ian moving about. If he cooked breakfast, she wouldn't be able to eat it.

He came through the glass door onto the balcony, leaning over to kiss her.

'Morning, sweetheart.'

She hated that he sounded so cheerful. It was going to be one of the most stressful days of her life.

A couple of hours later, they were in Ian's car on the way to the salon. Jo stared at her watch. They were running late. 'We should have left earlier.'

'It's not until this afternoon,' Ian said. 'I can't imagine how it will take all morning to get ready.' He drove into another lane. From behind, a car horn blared.

'Get stuffed,' Ian said. He shot her a glance. 'Everything's going to be fine, sweetie. Your mother will be nice to you, and your sister will boss you around, but you're used to that.'

Jo said nothing. How was she going to get home? Ian hadn't mentioned picking her up. She'd rather cut her throat than ask.

At last, they pulled into the kerb outside the salon. 'Give me the address of the reception,' Ian said. 'I'll pick you up at eleven.'

'I don't have a pen,' Jo said.

Ian fished a pen out of his jacket pocket and held out the back of his hand. 'Write it there,' he said, as if they were a couple of school kids.

Obediently, she wrote down the address, pressing down hard with the pen. Hopefully, it hurt.

She handed the pen back to him.

He dropped it into his jacket pocket then leaned forward and kissed her on the mouth.

His lips felt soft. Her body stirred. She wanted him more than ever, but she hated him.

Running a finger down the side of her face, he said, 'You'll be fine.'

Climbing out of the car, she walked towards the salon. Before she opened the door, she turned and looked back and he was still there, sitting in his car, watching. Her anger was so overwhelming she almost stuck up a finger at him. *Bastard*.

Inside the salon Renee, looking more pregnant than ever, inserted large pink rollers into sections of Maureen's hair. Kathleen waited in a chair, reading a copy of *Wuthering Heights*.

Maureen glared at Jo. 'You're late.'

'Sorry,' Jo said. 'The traffic was awful.'

'Hello, Jo,' Renee said. 'Lizzie, shampoo Jo's hair, please.'

Pale Lizzie said hello and led Jo over to a basin. She slung a black cape around Jo's shoulders, fastening it at the neck, and draped a small black towel over the top, securing it with a clip.

'I bet you're excited,' she said as she turned on the taps. 'Is this your first time as a bridesmaid?'

'Yes,' Jo said as Lizzie ran water over her hair with a hose. Her earlier nervousness had been replaced by a strange, floating sensation.

Lizzie squirted shampoo on Jo's wet hair. 'I can't wait to see you three all dressed up.' Her long fingers massaged shampoo into Jo's scalp. 'Maureen said your boyfriend's not coming.'

'No,' Jo said. Her mind automatically searched for an excuse but found none.

'You wouldn't have been able to spend much time with him anyway,' Lizzie said. 'You couldn't even sit together.'

It wasn't the point.

After Lizzie finished shampooing Jo's hair, she led her to an empty chair.

'Pop Maureen under the dryer, please,' Renee said to Lizzie as she rolled a set of trays holding plastic rollers towards Jo.

'I'll just do a quick trim,' Renee said, fishing a comb out of her pocket. She snipped at Jo's fringe.

'Not too short,' Jo said.

'Relax,' Renee said.

'When are you having the baby?' Jo asked.

'Three weeks. This is my last job before I leave.' Renee made a face. 'I can't think of anything worse than being a housewife. Chris is going to enclose our back verandah so I can have a salon at home and Mum's going to look after the baby a couple of days a week.'

'That sounds perfect,' Jo said.

'Maureen's going to do the same,' Renee said.

Jo felt a nasty little prickle of envy. A job at home *and* a baby.

When their hair was done, Maureen drove Jo and Kathleen to Noble Park in her pale green Volkswagen. 'There's heaps of people at home,' she said, occasionally flicking a glance at herself in the rear-vision mirror. 'Dad came this morning, and Robbie's there, and Mona and Simone. Uncle Seamus and Auntie Nora are staying, and Auntie Eileen, of course.'

'I've been banished from my room,' Kathleen said from the back seat. 'I've got to sleep on the couch. Auntie Eileen's in there, and Uncle Seamus and Auntie Nora are in your old room.'

'You do have to put yourself out now and then,' Maureen said.

Kathleen made a snorting noise. 'When have you ever done it?'

'Don't bicker,' Jo said. 'How are Mum and Dad?'

'They're staying well apart,' Kathleen said. 'When we left, Dad was in the shed with Uncle Seamus and Mum was with the women.'

'If he gets on the beers before the wedding, I'll murder him,' Maureen said.

'Don't be ridiculous. Dad never gets drunk.'

'Uncle Seamus does. He's a bad influence.'

Jo rolled her eyes. Maureen sounded exactly like Mum.

When they arrived at the house, Jo took a deep breath as she followed Maureen along the path to the front porch. This was going to be excruciating.

Maureen opened the front door to the smell of lemon-scented furniture polish and Simone's screams. They hurried into the kitchen, where Simone sat on Mona's lap while Monica crouched in front, dabbing at Simone's bloodstained knee with a wet face washer. Monica's hair was set into its usual helmet shape, but she looked smaller and thinner, less certain of herself.

'Hello, Jo,' she said.

She sounded friendly, as if she'd never told Jo she was no longer her daughter, nagged her to screaming point, or told her heaps of times that she looked cheap. Ian had been right; Jo had worked herself up for nothing. 'Hello, Mum,' she said.

Monica rinsed the bloodied face washer in a bowl of water and laid it back on Simone's knee. 'Thank goodness it doesn't need stitches.'

Robbie put platters of sandwiches on the table. 'Nice to see you, Jo. How about you girls have something to eat. It's going to be a long day.'

'Thanks, Rob.' Kathleen made a dive for the sandwiches, but Maureen said, 'No thanks.'

'How about a cup of tea?'

'Yes,' Maureen said. 'And a biscuit. Just the one. Thanks.'

Through the doorway into the living room, Jo spotted Auntie Nora standing at the ironing board, pressing Maureen's veil, which fell in folds to the carpet. She set the iron down and hooked the veil, embroidered with tiny daisies, onto a hanger.

'It's done,' she called.

'Lovely,' Maureen said. 'Thanks.'

Auntie Nora blew her a kiss.

'Where's Rufus and Auntie Eileen?' Jo asked.

'Taking him for a walk,' Monica said. She was bandaging Simone's knee after putting a soft pad on it.

The back door banged, and Jo's dad and her Uncle Seamus appeared. 'Hello, love.'

He looked thinner. Maybe he wasn't happy living in the caravan park.

Jo went over and hugged him. 'Dad.'

'My turn now,' Uncle Seamus said grinning, holding out his arms.

He was Jo's favourite uncle, large and always smiling. Why on earth had he married Auntie Nora? She always looked as if she could smell something bad.

Monica fixed Simone's bandage with a couple of small safety pins. 'There,' she said. 'You'll be fine now.'

She looked up at Kev and pointed to a plate. 'The cheese and pickle ones are over there.'

He nodded. 'Thanks.'

Jo watched Auntie Nora take the veil, some of it folded over one arm, through the glass doors into the hall, on her way to Maureen's bedroom.

The front door opened and closed and Auntie Eileen came in with Rufus. She took off his lead and he came bounding up to Jo, his plumed tail wagging.

Jo knelt and kissed his nose, letting him plaster her face with licks.

'How are you, dear?' Auntie Eileen asked.

'Fine,' Jo said. 'You?'

'Coping,' Auntie Eileen said.

Monica stood in the doorway. 'Don't let Rufus mess up your hair, Jo. You'd better go and get ready.'

As Jo went along the hall, Auntie Nora came out of Kathleen's room carrying a shirt on a hanger. She looked at Jo with an expression of disgust. 'You should be ashamed of yourself.'

Jo walked past. She didn't care what Auntie Nora thought.

Half an hour later, after Jo and Kathleen were ready, Maureen, wearing a silky bra, slip and panties, stepped into her wedding dress. Jo zipped her up and set the pillbox on top of her head, with the veil spread out around her.

'You look gorgeous,' Jo said, as Maureen peered at herself in the mirror.

Maureen smiled. 'Thanks.'

There was a knock on the door. 'Can I come in?' Monica asked. The door opened and she walked in, wearing a coral-coloured Thai silk dress and coat.

'You all look lovely,' she said. 'I'm so proud.'

Jo stared at her, shocked.

'She means it,' Maureen said. 'Don't you, Mum?'

She nodded. 'Yes. I know I don't say it very often.'

'You never say it,' Kathleen said.

Monica frowned. 'Well, I have now. I'd better go and check on your father. He's probably wearing odd shoes.'

...

Ian drove along the Nepean Highway. The look Jo had given him before she entered the salon was hard to forget. She hated him.

He knew he should have agreed to go, but the idea of watching Maureen getting married made his guts churn. She was everything he disliked in a woman. She wore too much make-up, swanned around like a low-grade film star, and bossed Jo. Worst of all, she'd flirted with him at the bowling alley. The only person Maureen cared about was herself.

The traffic lights at North Road turned red. Ian scowled. Damn it, he was going to get every red light on the way home. As his car slowed, he started thinking about Monica, who thought she was right about everything, including that he was a playboy. It made him angry, because at some level he knew she was right, or why else had he screwed that woman in the car park? But Monica was also wrong because playboys had no conscience, while afterwards he'd felt deeply ashamed. Ian frowned. He couldn't do anything about it. As Doug had said to him once, the past was the past, even though it kept rearing its ugly head in the present.

They'd had a few beers one night, after karate. Doug had told him that his father was a bastard. Once, when Doug was about six or seven, he'd climbed onto the roof of their house. His father had told him to jump, and he'd catch him. 'I jumped,' Doug said, 'but he just stood there. I broke my ankle. My father said, "that'll teach you never to trust anyone."

'I grew up thinking I was a piece of shit,' Doug continued, 'and I acted like it. But when I was twenty-six, I looked at myself and thought, *If I go on like this, he wins*. That was the day I changed.'

'My dad left when I was seven,' Ian said. 'I knew he beat Mum up, but I idolised him. I blamed her for him leaving. I wanted them back together. Must have had rocks in my head.'

Doug shook his head. 'No mate,' he said, 'You were a kid. Didn't understand.'

Ian swallowed some beer. 'Lucky for me, Mum's the forgiving sort.'

'Mine died,' Doug said. 'I can hardly remember her.'

'Is your dad still around?' Ian asked.

Doug nodded. 'Yeah. Lives in Grafton. I go up and see him now and then. He hasn't changed. Doesn't bother me anymore. He's the loser, not me.'

'I met Dad in the city one day,' Ian said. 'Worked out he didn't give a shit about me, or Tricia. I hate him.'

'Hate takes too much energy, mate. He's not worth it.'

The traffic lights turned green and the car in front of Ian's moved forward. At this rate, he'd be late for karate.

Chapter Twenty-seven

The photographer was a fidgety young man called Tom. While he was setting up his equipment in the living room, Jo fetched Maureen's bouquet of creamy gardenias and the white satin horseshoe, a present from Auntie Eileen. 'Every marriage needs a dose of good luck,' Auntie Eileen said as Maureen unwrapped it. Maureen had glanced at Jo. *What does she know?*

Robbie had brought over her fake antique chair, covered in dusty pink velvet, for the photographs. Tom, who had a habit of snapping his fingers when he wanted Maureen to look in a certain direction and saying, 'wonderful' or 'fab', took pictures of her sitting in the chair, her veil caught to one side and bunched at her feet. Then he took pictures of her with Kev, who looked smarter than he had for years in his dark suit, white shirt and buttonhole.

While this was happening, Jo imagined Ian at home, feet up on his horrible couch reading his new detective story, *The Deep Blue Goodbye*. He was doing exactly what he wanted while she'd be in St Anthony's enduring a nuptial mass and feeling totally abandoned.

Tom beckoned Jo, Kathleen and Simone over, and took pictures of them with Maureen, and to everyone's surprise, Simone did as she was told and sat cross-legged in front of the others holding a basket of flowers, her sore knee forgotten.

'Wonderful,' Tom said when he'd finished. 'Let's go outside.'

As they stepped onto the porch, a pair of black Ford mustangs decorated with white ribbons pulled in at the kerb. Almost immediately, the neighbours began to emerge from their houses and stood on their front porches.

At that moment, the swirling thoughts in Jo's mind disappeared and everything felt right, the aqua crepe dress soft on her skin, sunlight slanting across the lawn, the gentle whispering of leaves on the young trees. Maureen stood in front of the liquidambar, and Jo and Kathleen went forward to arrange her veil.

Afterwards, they piled into the cars and arrived at St Anthony's. After Tom took photos of Maureen and Kev exiting the car, they went inside. Monica stood in one of the front pews wearing her Thai silk dress and coat, and Auntie Eileen stood next to her in a canary yellow suit that clashed with her pink cheeks. Michael and his best man John stood in front of the altar, Michael as handsome as usual and John almost unrecognisable in his dark suit and neat haircut. Maureen had told Jo that John had been in a car accident in which his girlfriend had died. He was grief stricken, and she'd been worried he'd chicken out of the wedding. Jo stared at John's solemn face. He'd gone through something horrific, which made her dread of people's opinions about her seem pathetic.

During the mass she stood and knelt and murmured the responses, and when Maureen and Michael spoke their vows, Maureen said the words so quietly she could barely be heard, while Michael spoke his firmly and confidently. When he slipped the ring on Maureen's finger, he did it without a fumble. And as Jo watched him lift Maureen's veil for a kiss, her chest ached because it would never happen to her, and despite her anger, the thought of leaving Ian made her feel so wretched that tears filled her eyes, and a couple slid down her cheeks.

Kathleen pulled a hankie from the front of her dress and handed it to Jo, who pressed it to her eyes, hoping her fake eyelashes wouldn't peel off. She glanced across at the front pew and nearly everyone was watching Maureen and Michael, but Auntie Eileen was looking straight at her. *Be brave, Jo.*

Jo gulped and handed the hankie back to Kathleen, feeling an unexpected urge to giggle as Kathleen shoved it back down the front of her dress.

Later, when they all stood on the church steps, Jo remembered Ian's story about the priest running out with the register because he hadn't signed, and how desperately he'd wanted to run away, but when she looked at Maureen and Michael, they were smiling at each other as if the idea of running away would never enter their heads.

After Tom had taken more photos, they got into the Ford mustangs, except for Monica, who was travelling with Auntie Eileen, and Kev, who was with Uncle Seamus and Auntie Nora, and headed towards the Dandenongs.

As soon as Jo and Kathleen were in the car, Jo pulled her cigarettes from her handbag.

'Can I have one?' Kathleen asked.

Jo raised her eyebrows. 'Have you taken it up?'

'No,' Kathleen said. 'It's just a weird day. How come you were crying?'

Jo shrugged. 'It's a weird day.'

Kathleen took the cigarette Jo offered, and they both lit up.

'You should make sure you have a good time tonight,' Kathleen said. 'Guzzle champagne and dance with every handsome man that asks.'

Jo tapped ash from her cigarette. 'I might just do that.' She looked at Kathleen. 'Have you brought a good book?'

Kathleen's eyes gleamed. 'No, I thought I'd find a nice waiter and snog with him outside.'

The sound of their laughter filled the car.

...

When Ian arrived home from karate, he stripped the bed and bundled the sheets and pillowcases into a plastic laundry basket, then went into the kitchen and put on some coffee. Outside, a flock of birds soared across the sky.

Ian made his coffee and wandered into the living room. Paint charts lay on the coffee table. He picked them up. Jo had circled a couple of shades in pencil – a soft apricot, and shell pink. Before she moved in, he hadn't given a shit about the place, other than keeping it tidy, but she liked things to look nice. If the landlord agreed he'd paint the walls although he couldn't come at the pink. He'd even chuck out the couch if she asked. It wouldn't hurt for him to compromise a bit.

He put down the charts, sat on the couch and sipped his coffee. He'd promised to do everything he could to make Jo happy and he'd failed. She'd practically begged him to go to the wedding, but he'd let his prejudices take over. Weddings were bullshit. Marriage was a trap. His other failures came into his mind – the breakdown of his marriage, abandoning his daughter to be brought up by another man, flirting with women, and committing adultery. Christ, he was thinking like a Catholic. Why couldn't he give himself a break?

He recalled Doug's words. *If I keep on behaving like him he'll win.* Ian's mother sometimes said that in some ways, he was like his father. He hadn't walked out on Ange, but he'd made it easy for her to tell him to leave. He'd made it hard for Anna, just as his father had made it hard for him. Would he go on wrecking his life when he had the chance to build something special with Jo? How could he get over his fear that every relationship he had would fail? Ian drank his coffee, put the cup down on the coffee table. He had to face the fear, not give in to it. An idea came to him. Before his relationship with Jo, he would have laughed at himself for even thinking it. Now he knew it was exactly right.

...

The reception rooms were in Olinda, at the end of a long gravel drive, edged by rhododendrons with large pink blooms. Smooth lawns surrounded the building, and water cascaded from a stone fountain.

The wedding party gathered on the lawn under a spreading oak as Tom took pictures of Maureen and Michael in front of an archway of scented wisteria, followed by the rest of them until Jo's face ached from smiling, and Simone began to grizzle. At last, Tom said, 'Fab. All done,' and began to pack up his equipment.

Everyone went inside and sat at the top table, which was covered with a spotless white cloth ironed into neat rectangles. Several vases of striped carnations, accented with delicate ferns, were set along its length, and glassware and cutlery gleamed at each place.

As the guests came in and sat down, waiters emerged from a pair of doors at the back carrying embossed silver trays on which stood bottles of wine and beer.

Jo sat next to Maureen, with John on her other side. She had no idea what to say to him. The word sorry would sound pathetic. He'd nodded at her but said nothing. When a waiter offered them drinks, John chose beer, and Jo a glass of white wine. She tilted the glass to her lips and looked across the room at the guests sitting at the round tables. All of them were with their husband, wife, fiancé, boyfriend or girlfriend except for her and Auntie Eileen, who sat with the two sets of parents nearby.

John drank his beer and set his empty glass on the table with a clunk. 'How are you, Jo?'

Dark shadows lay under his eyes. Maybe he wasn't sleeping, or drinking too much, or a combination of the two.

'I'm mad as hell.' She was appalled at herself. 'Sorry, I shouldn't have said that.'

John shrugged. 'People are pussyfooting around me and I'm sick of it. Say what you want.'

She fiddled with her knife and fork. 'My boyfriend wouldn't come today.'

'The one you live with.'

'I only have one boyfriend,' she said.

'Sorry, I didn't mean you had other boyfriends.'

It felt weird him telling her he was sorry.

A waiter came up and poured more beer into John's glass. 'I didn't want to come either, but Michael's my best mate,' John said. 'I couldn't let him down.'

Jo straightened her knife and fork. 'That's really nice of you.'

Food waiters put seafood cocktails in front of them.

John stabbed at a prawn with his fork. 'Your boyfriend should have come.'

Jo looked at his stubby fingers and hoped that one day another girl would fall in love with him, and they'd be happy. She blinked away tears, and luckily, John hadn't noticed, he was drinking more beer.

The food arrived, a choice of chicken or steak, roast vegetables and peas, followed by apple pie and cream, and afterwards, the speeches, in which Michael surprised everyone with how good his was, until he made them laugh by admitting he'd been practising for months. When it was John's turn he talked about how he and Michael had been at school together since they were six, played footy and cricket and worked with each other, so he reckoned he probably saw more of him than Maureen did, and she was a lucky woman to have him. Everyone laughed again, and Jo's Auntie Eileen laughed louder than anyone else.

The music started, and Maureen and Michael waltzed on the polished parquet floor as people clapped, and then it was everyone else's turn, but no-one asked Jo to dance, and John sat beside her drinking beer, so she joined Simone and Mona, who were dancing by themselves at the edge of the floor. When she eventually got back to the table, John had vanished. She looked around, and spotted him outside on the terrace, which was strung with lights.

Picking up her handbag, she walked past Kathleen, who was dancing with the other groomsman, and her mum who was talking with Michael's mother, and her dad who was talking with Michael's father, and went through the glass doors onto the terrace. John stood at the far end, looking into the darkened garden.

'Hello,' she said.

He turned. 'It's you.'

The air felt cold. She shivered.

'Here.'

John took off his jacket and she wrapped it around her shoulders.

'I had to get out of there,' he said. 'Or I'd keep drinking.'

Jo opened her handbag for her cigarettes.

He pulled a packet out of his suit jacket. 'Have one of mine.'

She took one and he pulled out his lighter and leaned forward. His shirt glimmered white, and he smelt of beer. He had a stocky build, like her ex-boyfriend Robert.

'Everyone's in there having a good time,' John said. 'And I'm out here wondering why Deanna died instead of me.'

'I'm sorry,' Jo said.

John lit his own cigarette and blew out smoke 'Your being sorry doesn't make any difference. I really loved her, but I wish she'd never gone out with me.' He turned to face the garden, staring into the dark. 'I wanted to ask you out once, but Maureen said you were with a loser from Carnegie.'

'I was,' Jo said.

'Now you're living with someone who won't even come to a wedding with you. I don't get it. I'm going for a walk. Need to clear my head.'

'I'll come with you.'

'Why?' John asked.

'I don't know,' she said.

'I don't need saving.'

She wasn't sure what he meant.

They set off across the lawn. A dew had fallen, and in minutes, Jo's feet felt cold and damp. Her satin shoes would be ruined. She remembered the night when Ian had driven past two crumpled cars at the side of the road. He'd told her to make the most of life before it was too late. It sounded easy, but it was hard. She'd thought if they loved each other they'd be happy, but that was before she knew about his past, and being called a slut at Maureen's kitchen tea, and feeling resentful that Jenny was getting presents while she got none. But now, none of that mattered. When Ian came to pick her up tonight, she'd tell him about John and his girlfriend, and how it had made her realise there was nothing she could do if her parents decided not to get back together, or prejudiced people said nasty things about her. And she was going to tell the people at work they were living together because she no longer wanted to hide it.

'Her family wouldn't have me at the funeral,' John said. 'I don't even know where she's buried.'

'Would it help if you did?' Jo asked.

'I don't know.'

They'd reached the drive. Gravel crunched under their shoes as they walked past the rhododendrons towards the entrance. Stars glittered high above.

A pair of lights appeared at the gate moving slowly towards them. Jo put her hand on John's arm and pulled him to the side of the drive as the car slowed and stopped. Her breath caught as she recognised Ian's car.

The passenger window rattled as it was wound down and Ian's face appeared in the gap. 'You two trying to hitch a ride?'

His voice sounded light, but she knew he was furious.

'John,' she said, 'This is Ian, my boyfriend.'

Beside her, John said, 'So you're the bastard that wouldn't come to the wedding.'

Ian got out of the car, slamming the door. As he stormed in front of the headlights, she saw he was wearing a suit, shirt and tie. Did he think she was out here to kiss and cuddle with John? It was ridiculous and sad that he should believe it. 'John's drunk,' she said. 'Please.'

Ian stopped. His voice was cold. 'What are you doing out here?'

Her insides seemed to wither. 'I'll tell you later,' she said.

'Tell me now.'

'He's drunk,' she repeated.

'So, you go out into the dark with every drunk you find, do you?' Ian said.

Across the lawn, faint music issued from the reception centre.

'I know him,' Jo said.

'Ex-boyfriend, is he?'

'No, he's Michael's best man.'

'Michael's my best mate,' John said.

'Well, you can piss off.'

Something inside Jo snapped. 'Don't talk to him like that. You don't know anything.'

'I thought I could trust you.'

Jo's frustration threatened to explode. Didn't he realise how much she loved him?

John swayed forward. 'Look, mate, you've got it wrong. She's out here 'cause she thinks I'm gonna top myself. I'm not. Wouldn't be right.'

'His girlfriend died,' Jo said.

Ian stared at John, then at Jo and nodded a couple of times, as if to convince himself. He held out his hand to John. 'Sorry. I've been a prick. Got the wrong end of the stick.' He turned to Jo. 'I'm sorry, sweetheart. I should have known you'd never do that.'

She glared at him. 'No, I wouldn't.'

'Need a leak,' John said, and staggered off into the dark.

'Wait.' Jo slipped John's jacket off her shoulders, but he'd disappeared.

Ian took the jacket from her and tossed it onto the back seat of his car. The cold was stealing into Jo's bones.

'Here,' Ian said, taking off his own jacket and wrapping it around her.

Jo inhaled the warmth. 'You weren't s'posed to come 'til eleven.'

'I changed my mind. I thought I'd sneak into the reception and ask you to dance. Will you dance with me now?'

She stared at him in surprise. It was like a scene from one of those old-fashioned films she'd watched as a kid, but they were standing on a gravel drive in the middle of the night, and it was real.

He took her hand. 'I love you,' he said. 'I can't do without you, and I don't know where it'll end, but that's it.'

She felt as light as air, the luckiest girl alive.

He took her in his arms, and they danced on the damp grass under the stars, and she thought of Maureen in her beautiful wedding dress, and Michael in his dark suit, dancing on the polished parquet of the reception centre and felt no envy, just a certainty that everything between her and Ian would be fine, because they loved each other.

John staggered out of the dark. 'Can you give me a lift to the station, mate? I wanna go home.'

'Say yes,' Jo said in Ian's ear.

'Where do you live?' Ian asked.

'Dandenong.'

'We'll drive you there.'

'Thanks mate, appreciate it.'

They helped John into the car, but before Jo got in, she looked across the lawn at the lit-up reception rooms. Inside, people would be drinking, and dancing, and her mum would be feeling proud that a daughter of hers had married a good Catholic boy. Later, a girl would squeal as she caught Maureen's bouquet, and when Maureen was getting changed, she'd realise that Jo had gone. Then people would notice that John had gone too, and tongues would wag, but Jo didn't care, she and Ian were together.

Acknowledgements

Thank you to Jess, Sinead, Meg and Zalia at Hembury Books. You are the best! Thanks to Jossi Clyde, Chris Young, Sherryn Hind, Lizz Sayers, Kelly Teitzel and Matt Elsbury, fellow writers since 2012, and to Kate Ryan, my marvellous mentor, who kept urging me to not hold back.

And as always to my lovely extended family, Adam, Holly, Meaghan, Dave, Chris, Lauren, Milly, Callum, Nathan and Bodie.

www.ingramcontent.com/pod-product-compliance
Lightning Source LLC
Chambersburg PA
CBHW031957180726
48283CB00008B/2471